BRASS
DRAGON CODEX

Books by R.D. Henham

RED DRAGON CODEX

BLACK DRAGON CODEX

GREEN DRAGON CODEX
June 2009

WHITE DRAGON CODEX
January 2010

BLUE DRAGON CODEX
March 2011

BRONZE DRAGON CODEX

BRASS DRAGON CODEX

SILVER DRAGON CODEX
September 2009

GOLD DRAGON CODEX
September 2010

COPPER DRAGON CODEX
September 2011

BRASS
DRAGON CODEX

R.D. Henham

MIRRORSTONE

Brass Dragon Codex

©2009 Wizards of the Coast, Inc.

Text by R.D. Henham with assistance from Rebecca Shelley
Cover art by Vinod Rams
Interior art by Todd Lockwood
Cartography by Dennis Kauth
First Printing: January 2009

9 8 7 6 5 4 3 2 1

Library of Congress Cataloging-in-Publication Data

Henham, R. D.
    Brass dragon codex / R.D. Henham.
        p. cm.
    "Mirrorstone."
    Summary: An orphaned brass dragon named Kyani befriends a gnome and through their friendship, both become better listeners.
        ISBN 978-0-7869-5108-6
    [1. Dragons--Fiction. 2. Gnomes--Fiction. 3. Fantasy.] I. Title.
    PZ7.H3884Br 2009
    [Fic]--dc22

                                                                    2008026329

ISBN: 978-0-7869-5108-6
620-23974720-001-EN

U.S., CANADA,   EUROPEAN HEADQUARTERS
ASIA, PACIFIC, & LATIN AMERICA   Hasbro UK Ltd
Wizards of the Coast, Inc.   Caswell Way
P.O. Box 707   Newport, Gwent NP9 0YH
Renton, WA 98057-0707   GREAT BRITAIN
+1-800-324-6496   Save this address for your records.

Visit our Web site at www.mirrorstonebooks.com

To all my wonderful assistants who work so hard
to make the Dragon Codices possible.

—R.D.H.

To Harmony Shelley, my little Kyani,
a brass dragon in human form if there ever was one.

—R.S.

Dear Honored Scribe Henham,

I must say, you have an incredibly competent messenger. I'm currently hidden in a hastily built tree house raised in a rather tall fir tree in the middle of a vast Solamnic forest, and yet he found me with seemingly no trouble at all. I hope you pay him well!

Enclosed is my next bundle of notes. They are all about a brass dragon I met back in the desert in northern Solamnia—that same chatty brass dragon I mentioned when last I wrote.

As it turns out, this brass dragon (named Kyani) recently encountered a crafty gnome named Hector. Hector, being a gnome and all, is determined to invent incredible new mechanical devices—or kill himself in a fabulously large explosion while trying. His most recent idea was to create a fancy new communication device to help the citizens of a once-lost city communicate with faraway towns almost instantly—without magic!

At first, people dismissed Hector's invention talk as typical gnome ramblings. But as he set about proving his device would work, he quickly drew the attention of dwarves, knights, thieves, and more—all who wanted the device as their own! Throw in our friend Kyani, and it adds up to a mighty big adventure for good ol' Hector.

You'll find that my notes this time are rather extensive—Kyani sure loves to talk (and talk . . . and talk), so there are a lot of neat details for you to pore over as you put together the tale for the rest of the world to read. In the meantime, I'd best get ready to continue my journey—I've heard word of a green dragon down south who is causing quite a stir, and I must investigate!

All my best,
Sindri Suncatcher
Esteemed Collector of Dragon Tales,
Anecdotes, Narratives, Stories, and Yarns

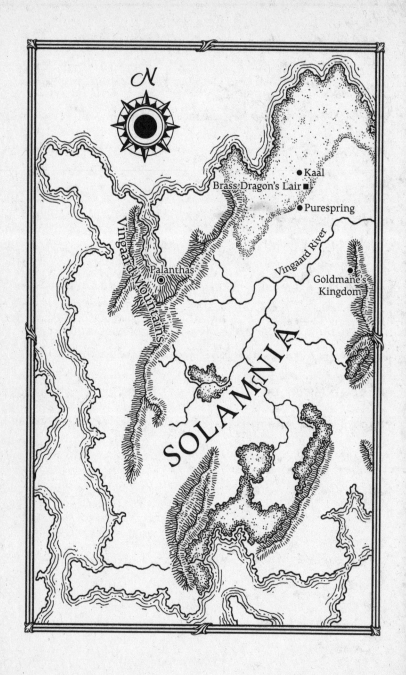

PROLOGUE

Kyani paced the Grand Conversation Hall, his claws clicking against the marble floor, his tail lashing back and forth. His stomach growled, and he rippled his brass wings in agitation.

"There now, you see," he said, as if his parents were with him in the vast chamber. "I'm starving, and where are you? Gone off for days now. And you told me to stay here and wait. Don't even poke my nose out of the lair until you come back. But no, no. You didn't come back, did you? No you didn't, and I'm stuck here all alone, starving."

Kyani let out a petulant roar and climbed the steps into the Hall of Art. He padded among his parents' treasures. A huge tapestry, stitched with green and gold thread, showed a landscape thick with trees and flowers. A stream of sparkling blue water swept down through the forested scene.

He shook his head at it. "You can't be real," he said. "That many trees? So green? And running water like that, it would evaporate in a day or two."

He stomped past an artistically twisted ancient tree branch. "So beautiful," he said, sniffing the dead piece of wood. He snaked his long tongue out to lick it. The wood tasted dry and sweet.

His stomach rumbled again, and he shook his head. His parents' treasures couldn't fill his stomach. Well, maybe they could, but his parents would never forgive him for eating their valuables.

"Alone," he grumbled. "So alone. No one to talk to. Where are they? Where have they gone? Do you know?" he asked the tree branch.

"How should I know?" he answered for the wood, making his voice sound low and raspy.

"Well you should know," he yelled at the branch. "And you"—he kicked a bolt of shimmering blue material—"fine lot of help you are."

"Ouch. Don't kick me," he said in a high, squeaky voice that he imagined the material would speak in.

He kicked it again. "Oh, be quiet, or I'll eat you."

The blue material fell silent.

He walked the length of the hall, licking a porcelain vase on one side, sniffing an oil painting of a sunrise on the other.

"Yum." He snatched it up in his jaws, and then set it down unharmed.

Imitating his father's deep voice, Kyani growled, "That is a priceless painting commissioned by Astinus himself. Irreplaceable."

Kyani snarled at it, then stormed out of the hall into the tunnel on the far side. He tucked his wings tight against his back, stuck out his long neck, and strode toward one of the lair's many bolt-hole exits.

"Wait here, Kyani," he called, imitating his mother's worried tones. "Stay inside. Stay safe."

"Stay here," he muttered. "I can't stay here forever all alone." His voice rumbled down the empty corridor. *Alone . . . Alone . . .* He slumped to the ground and laid his head on his front legs.

The smell of desert heat came from the end of the tunnel. Golden light filtered through the sand that covered the entrance. "What if something happened to them?" he whispered. "What if they're not coming back? What if they need my help?"

He jumped to his feet. "I'm coming," he roared. He lumbered forward and burst through the sand, out into the desert heat.

The sun blazed overhead, warming his scales. So nice. Behind him, three tall red and orange sandstone spires marked the rock formation that hid his lair. The scent of sage and creosote bushes wafted up across the sand to him. A scorpion skittered away into a hole at the base of a tall green cactus.

"Nice to meet you too," he said to the scorpion. "And hello to you," he greeted the cactus. "And good morning, sunshine." He spread his wings, basking in the light.

Out across the sand, a vulture screamed and took to the air, leaving behind a lump of something on the ground.

"Hey, come back and talk to me," he yelled at the bird. The vulture circled in the pale blue air.

"I wonder what that is," Kyani said, taking a step toward the sand-covered lump.

Don't come out, no matter what you hear or smell. His father's command echoed in his mind. *Stay inside until we come for you.*

Kyani scanned the sky for danger, but saw only the vulture. Here and there across the sand, a tuft of yellow grass poked up beside a clump of sage or thistle. A breeze broke one of the thistles free, and it tumbled past Kyani's snout and came to a stop against a nearby cactus.

Frowning, Kyani sniffed the air. The new wind direction brought him the smell of decaying flesh, and beneath that, his mother's faint, tangy metallic scent.

Roaring, he rushed forward to the lump of sand. Blood spotted the ground where the vulture had been feasting. Kyani pawed the sand off the lump to reveal glittering brass scales.

"Mother!" Kyani cried. A long gash, made by a claw that must have been twice as big as his father's, cut down one of her sides. Black scorch marks darkened her scales.

Overhead, the vulture screamed and flew away.

"Mother?" Kyani nudged her, begging her to respond,

though the stench of death hung over her. His belly burned, his hunger replaced with sorrow.

"She's dead," he moaned. Grief paralyzed him. He sank to the sand beside her.

Far off in the distance, he saw another lump. Bigger. He smelled more death. He smelled his father. His parents would never come back to the lair again.

A shadow brushed the sun. Kyani sniffed. He felt he should say something, tell his parents good-bye, but his throat constricted and nothing came out. A patch of darkness appeared on the sand and moved in his direction. The wind carried a thunderstorm smell.

Blue glinted in the sunlight above.

Kyani jumped to his feet just as an ancient blue dragon swooped at him and shot a lightning bolt in his direction. The bolt hit the sand next to Kyani, melting it to glass. Kyani scrambled away, shuddering with the thought of that deadly bolt touching his scales.

Now he understood the scorch marks on his mother. Now he knew what had torn her side. The blue dragon was twice his father's size—it was a great wyrm. Kyani might barely reach to one of his knees.

The blue dragon lifted higher into the sky and made a slow, lumbering turn to come at him again.

Kyani scrambled for the lair's hidden entrance.

Chapter One

The burning sand swept around two lone figures beneath the hot sun—one a gnome only three feet tall, the other a metal giant that towered five stories above the desert floor.

"Today is the day I conquer the giant," Hector said, staring up at the figure in front of him.

The giant's feet, legs, torso, arms, and head were all made out of bronze. The metal was not just armor, it *was* the whole giant, a huge, undefeatable mechanical creation. Not so long ago it had smashed through the city gates out into the desert and killed hundreds of people. Its mad rampage had ended when the magic artifact that controlled it had been crushed.

Now it stood unmoving not far from Kaal, the desert city it had almost destroyed.

Hector scratched his bald head. He'd just as soon leave it that way, but for his friend Amber, he'd face the giant and bring it back to life.

Square shadows played across the ground from the scaffolding that rose up to the giant's chest. Sand whispered over Hector's sandals, tickling his feet. Behind him, the huge gates that provided entrance through Kaal's massive sandstone walls creaked open.

Hector's heart leaped, and he shoved his hands into his leather apron pockets and turned in time to see Amber lead a donkey and cart toward him. He smiled as the sunlight glimmered off her tawny hair.

She stepped out briskly in front of the donkey, dragging it along and waving to Hector. A gold bracelet on her wrist tinkled as she waved. Fashioning the bracelet's little gold hummingbird charms had taken Hector quite a while, but for Amber it was worth it.

In the wagon sat a large metal clockwork mechanism that had taken Hector and Amber even more time to build than a few hummingbirds.

Behind the wagon strode Shem, the city leader—human, of course. There weren't too many gnomes out here in the desert, just Hector and Amber. Shem's face was tanned and lined from living under the desert sun his whole life. He wore loose-fitting silk clothing the color of sand. Fancy embroidery on the sleeves showed his status. His salt-and-pepper hair absorbed the sun, while Amber's glowed in it.

Hector gripped the wrench in his pocket with one

hand and waved to Amber and Shem with the other as they came toward him to the feet of the Bronze Giant.

"Stop right here, Thistle," Amber said, patting the donkey. "Hello, Hector. Shem and the city guard helped me load this, just like you said they would. Do you have the harness ready to lift it up there?"

"Yes. All ready. Thanks, Shem," Hector said.

Shem smiled and nodded, but his smile faded as he stared at the giant. "You sure you'll be able to control this thing? We just got the city walls rebuilt. I can see how fixing it could be a great asset to our defenses like you suggest, but . . ." Shem grimaced.

"We can control it. Absolutely." Hector grabbed the rope harness that hung down from the scaffolding and went to the heavy iron clockwork in the wagon. "You see, after we wind up the clockwork, I will set the lever to tell it how to move when we let it go. We'll be in complete control."

Shem's brow furrowed while Hector talked. "Slow down. Don't talk so fast," he said. "I didn't understand half of that. Oh, never mind, just show me."

"Will do." Hector motioned to Amber, and she climbed onto the clockwork. He pulled a lever that released a big bundle of bricks overhead on the other end of the harness rope. The weight of the falling bundle shot Amber and the clockwork into the air. Hector grabbed onto the harness as it passed over his head and rose with them. He whooped with delight as the air whipped across his bald head from the speed of the ride. Amber's voice joined his in the fun.

The clockwork came to a wobbling halt near the top of the scaffolding. Hector swung himself up onto the sturdy wood planks and gave Amber a hand off the clockwork.

Amber opened a large plate in the giant's chest. Still using the counterweight below to hold the heavy mechanism, Hector pulled the rope, guiding the clockwork into the open chest cavity. He had to push aside a web of bronze tubes to secure it into the place where the giant's original heart had been.

Three magic items had once powered and controlled the giant—the Heart of Purespring, the Bloodfire Rubies, and the Medallion of Awareness. The Heart had sat in the giant's chest and pumped the Bloodfire Rubies through the tubes, making the giant go, while the Medallion of Awareness controlled the giant. Too bad Kaal's enemies had stolen the medallion from Shem and turned the giant against its own city.

Hector didn't blame Shem for being nervous. If the great warrior Catriona hadn't smashed the medallion, Kaal's inhabitants would have been dead or enslaved instead of living in peace now.

When the fighting ended, Shem had let Catriona take the Heart back to her village, Purespring, where for hundreds of years it had pumped healing waters up to the therapeutic pools that pilgrims traveled long miles to experience. The Bloodfire Rubies went to Goldmane, the dwarf prince who was their rightful owner.

With the giant's magic gone, that left Hector and Amber to come up with an alternate way to animate it.

"That's got it," Hector said, tightening down the last bolt.

Amber clapped her hands with delight and reached for the crank. She gave Hector an excited smile. "This is it. The moment I've waited for all my life. We will animate the giant, and my Life Quest will be complete."

Hector smiled too. He knew the burn of a Life Quest, the all-consuming need to create the invention that was a gnome's sole purpose for living. Every gnome had their own Life Quest, and none could rest until they accomplished it. Amber had spent years back home in Haggersmoore tinkering with small mechanical creatures: an iron cat, a bird that flapped its wings and chirped, a little metal gnome that marched back and forth across the floor—all of them children's toys compared to the Bronze Giant.

Hector grabbed the crank along with Amber and heaved with all his might. It clattered and groaned as it turned, winding up the giant. He pulled and pushed until each turn made his muscles scream in protest. Sweat dripped down his face and into his eyes, but he couldn't let go to wipe it away. Not yet.

With one final squeal, the crank ground to a halt. Using all his weight to hold the crank down, Hector reached over with his foot and pushed the lever that would direct the clockwork to move the giant's right arm.

"All right, let go," Hector cried. He and Amber fell back, and the crank gave a loud squeal and spun. Amber landed on Hector's lap, and he hugged her as the clockwork turned and the gears moved.

With a shuddering groan, the giant's right thumb and index finger spread apart, one inch, two inches, three.

The gears spun down, and the giant stopped moving.

"We did it!" Hector shouted, jumping to his feet. "Did you see that? The giant moved. It really moved!"

Amber frowned as she dusted herself off.

Hector's joy faded. He didn't care if the giant moved or not. He just wanted Amber to be happy. "What's wrong? We did it!"

Amber shook her head. "It only moved three inches. All that work and it hardly moved at all. To really make the giant go we'll need a much bigger clockwork, one so big it wouldn't even fit in the giant's chest, and something a lot stronger than we are to wind it up." She punched the giant's chest panel in frustration, filling the air with a hollow gong. "It's just not practical. We'll have to think of some other invention to make it move."

Hector groaned. After so much work, they'd have to start all over.

CHAPTER TWO

Hector looped his leather apron over his head and tied it tight around his middle. He blinked bleary eyes at his cluttered work table, picked up a cog, set it back down, shoved aside a coil of copper wire, and spread out his drawing of a semaphore system that Shem had rejected.

Snores from Amber's room at the side of the lab filled the silence.

Hector trimmed the lamp to get more light. The flame sputtered, adding the scent of burning kerosene to the heavy smell of machine oil in the room. Dead-of-night darkness hung outside.

He grimaced and pushed aside the drawing. It had seemed like such a good idea, but everything was too dry out here in the desert. Sun and sand and more sand, and only a little water in a few places. That had been Shem's main objection to the semaphore system—no water for the operators while they sat in little buildings across the desert waiting to send the messages.

Hector rubbed his hands along his bald head. Once, he'd had plenty of hair to tug when faced with an obstacle to his inventions. But that had all been burned off in a fire he'd barely escaped.

He smiled as he thought of his friend Mudd, who'd been there with him. Mudd had gotten out unharmed, thanks to Hector. But the two had been separated in the process and never saw each other again.

A soft thump sounded from Amber's room, and she stumbled into the lab, rubbing her eyes. Her bracelet jingled with the movement. Her tawny hair stood up on her head in wild disarray.

"It's the middle of the night, Hector. What in the world are you doing? Not working on a communication device again, I hope? You need sleep as much as I do."

Hector grimaced. "Amber, go back to sleep. I'm working here. I promise I'll help you come up with a new way to animate the Bronze Giant in the morning." Hector grabbed a piece of paper and picked up a stick of charcoal.

Amber still stared at him. "I know perfecting a communication machine is your Life Quest, but these new device ideas are crazier than your flying invention."

Hector threw the charcoal onto the table, where it knocked over a beaker of acid. "Hey, my flying invention was a great idea. If people could fly, they could send messages much faster than walking or riding. Besides, it worked. It saved me from the fire. It's not my fault it got broken in a windstorm and I can't remember how to make it. The blueprints are back home in Haggersmoore."

He shuddered. The terrible sandstorm that had blown him across the desert and left him to die near Kaal still haunted his dreams. If Shem hadn't taken him in and helped him, he would not have survived. If he could make a good communication system, it might in small part pay Shem back as well as fulfill Hector's Life Quest.

Amber moved to clean up the spill before the acid ate through anything important or ignited something dangerous. "Fine. Stay up all night if you want. Just make sure you're awake to help me with the Bronze Giant in the morning." She threw down the acid-soaked towel and went back to her room.

Hector rubbed his nose to block out the smell of the acid, which had burned into the wooden table. Anger and frustration welled up inside him. When he'd been at home, most of his time had been consumed by helping with his father's Life Quest to build an invincible weapon. He thought he'd escaped all that. Here in the desert he thought he could work on his own Life Quest, but Amber just couldn't leave the Bronze Giant alone.

Hector paced to her doorway and looked in at her curled up on the bed. His face burned, and he gripped the door frame until his fingernails dug into the wood.

The first time he'd seen Amber in Haggersmoore, where they'd grown up, she'd taken his breath away with her hair, her face, her brilliance, and her inventiveness. She could think something up, plan it, and build it faster than any other gnome he'd ever met. Just being around her made him giddy.

The hummingbird bracelet glinted in the faint light from the lamp in the other room. She'd been so delighted when he gave it to her. He'd been happy as well, willing to give her anything—including his help with the Bronze Giant. But she just didn't understand his Life Quest. She wouldn't listen to him no matter how much he tried to explain his communication device ideas.

Hector turned back to the workbench. If only they had the same Life Quest, things would be perfect. Still, she was worth it, worth staying up all night to work on his own things so he could be with her during the day. Perhaps in the morning they'd think of a new way to get the giant moving.

Amber scurried through the city streets with her hands deep in her apron pockets, clutching her tools to make sure they didn't bounce out while she ran. Her feet padded across the street's colorful geometric stones.

The sun glimmered off the copper-flecked buildings around her, lingering on the runes that covered balconies and walls and flashing from the bronze minarets that topped the tallest buildings. The taste of her morning oatmeal clung to her tongue. She'd downed it in a few swallows after discovering Hector had already left their lab.

A flock of desert quail peeped as she raced through an alley and scattered them. From a window above, a human woman scolded her. Amber kept going, out into a main street, dodging between big people's legs, running under a wagon that lumbered across her path, and coming up panting at the city's edge.

The massive sandstone wall that surrounded Kaal towered above her, fifty feet tall and twenty feet wide at the base, crowned at the top with crenellated battlements and watchtowers. The wall could withstand large-scale attacks and keep out anything except the sand, which worked its way past and into clothes and shoes and houses. A strong sandstorm could whip over the walls and down the city streets, destroying every living thing not indoors.

Amber shook the thought away and hurried to the huge gates. She had vague memories of waking in the night and scolding Hector. She winced, fingering her bracelet. She hadn't meant to do it. Hector was her best friend. She shouldn't treat him like that.

From the gate she could see the Bronze Giant towering above the sand where she and Hector had left it the day before—the fingers of its right hand spread those measly three inches. Sunlight glimmered off its bronze armor. A black dot, which from a distance looked like a fly, moved along the scaffolding against the giant's open chest cavity. Hector. He'd worked through the night and still beaten her out to the giant.

A knot formed in the pit of her stomach, and she feared she'd made Hector angry.

She raced across the hot sand to the giant. A gnome-sized basket sat next to the scaffolding. She climbed in and tripped a lever, releasing the bundle of bricks far overhead. The bricks fell and the basket shot up just like the clockwork had the previous day.

The basket jerked to a stop against the scaffold where Hector stood. Amber rolled out, two wrenches and a screwdriver falling from her apron as she did. She scrambled to pick them up while greeting Hector.

"Morning," Hector said without looking at her.

Amber got to her feet and saw him fiddling with the clockwork. She shoved her tools into her apron and cleared her throat. Fixing the giant was too big of a job for her to do alone. She needed Hector. Besides, he was her friend, and she hadn't meant to hurt his feelings.

"I'm sorry about last night," she said.

Hector accepted her apology with half a nod. "I think I've got this now. I've added several more gears and a lever, which will maximize the potential energy from the clockwork." He turned the crank. It moved around with a low grating noise, shaking the scaffold. He wound and wound until the sweat dripped down his face, soaking his shirt and making a glimmering sheen across his leather apron. His eyes stayed focused on the mechanism. The crank turned slower and slower until he couldn't budge it at all.

Amber reached up beside him and put her weight into it too. Finally, the crank wound as far as it could go. Hector reached around Amber and pulled the lever that would direct the clockwork to move the giant's legs.

"All right, let go," Hector said.

Amber let go and stepped back along with Hector. They both watched as the clockwork started up and the gears turned. With a shuddering groan, the giant's foot lifted a few inches off the ground. The gears spun down and the foot thundered back onto the sand.
Amber let out an exasperated breath.

Hector frowned, gripping the crank in frustration. "I was sure that would make it walk."

Amber forced herself to smile. "Thank you, Hector," she said, touching his arm. "I know you've done everything you can. Maybe it's hopeless. The giant is just too big to work this way."

Chapter Three

Hector dropped his hand from the crank. Amber was right. Their mechanism was too small to power the giant. Wind whispered through the desert sand below him, shifting it about in eddies. He licked his lips and rubbed his head, picturing how the Heart of Purespring must have worked.

The Heart went into the giant's chest and was hooked up with bronze tubes. The Bloodfire Rubies had gone into the Heart, which had pumped them through the tubes. That had started the giant. But it made no mechanical sense. Something magical had been involved, but Hector was no wizard.

The problem tugged at his mind.

He knew the Heart could pump water. That's what it did for the people of Purespring—pumped water at the edge of the desert to keep their village alive and to fill the pools of water that held healing properties. But inside the giant, it had pumped the rubies. Why rubies?

Why not oil or some other lubricant, conspicuously absent from the Bronze Giant? Beyond the obvious metaphor of blood, Hector could see no reason for them.

He fingered the bronze tube that had been so hard to get the rubies out of. But where had they gone while they were in the giant? Time to find out.

Ignoring Amber's demands to know what he was doing, Hector crawled into the giant, squeezing his body into the chest cavity between the tubes, wires, and gears. He kept his hand on the main bronze tube and followed it down into the giant's belly.

Heat from the desert sunlight baked the inside of the giant. Sweat covered Hector, making it easier to slide among the parts and follow the tube down. His head pounded, and he grew dizzy from the heat. He strained to see in the dim light from the cavity above.

The hose emptied into a clear glass container that sat on a ceramic plate nestled in the giant's pelvis. Two round cylinders rose on either side of Hector. The strong smell of acid wafted up from the giant's barrel legs, making Hector cough. So there was some kind of fluid in the giant after all, but why acid?

Covering his mouth with one hand, he ran the other hand along one of the cylinders. It was made from three substances stacked in sequence over and over again—a copper disk, a zinc disk, and a thick wad of blotting paper.

The other cylinder was identical, and in between them was the plate that had held the rubies.

Hector leaned forward and pressed on the plate. It moved downward under his weight like a scale. Gears creaked, and the cylinders lowered into the giant's legs. Hector yelped as he lost his perch against the moving cylinders. Pulling his weight back from the plate, he flailed to keep himself from falling.

As soon as he released his weight, the cylinders came back up to their former places.

"What are you doing down there?" Amber's worried voice reverberated down to him. "Are you all right?"

"I'm fine," he called, his heart racing. The heat and the fumes from the acid stung his eyes. He could hardly breathe, but he'd found something important. There was no way he'd leave without exploring the full implications.

Clutching the bronze tube that had funneled the rubies into the glass container, Hector let himself down onto the plate. It sank beneath him. Gears turned, and the cylinders once again lowered into the acid in the legs.

With a grinding creak they thunked into place. The smell of ozone filled the cavity, and lightning sprang up the wires from the cylinders and passed on to the clockwork heart above. A terrible hum rumbled through the giant. In his surprise, Hector's grip slipped from the bronze tubes to the glass container.

Then the giant moved.

Groaning and shuddering, it lifted its leg. The movement tilted Hector to the side, but his grip on the glass container kept him perched on the plate. *Thump.* The leg came down and the other lifted.

"It's working!" Hector yelled. "It's walking!"

Above him Amber screamed as the giant tore away from the scaffolding where she stood. Hector's heart froze. She'd fall. She'd die. He hadn't thought of that, hadn't known putting weight on the ceramic disk would give the giant enough power to move. He let go of the glass container and tried to jump off the disk, but the giant's movement made him lose his balance and sent him crashing back down.

The giant lumbered forward, the gears from Hector's clockwork telling it how to move. The motion from each giant stride sent Hector's stomach up into his throat.

Noxious fumes rose from the acid in the giant's legs. Lightning sizzled around Hector. His skin prickled. He almost laughed when he pictured his hair standing on end—only he didn't have any. But the lightning that powered the giant passed around him.

"Hector!" Amber's scream echoed down from above. She must have jumped into the open chest cavity when the giant started moving. He was relieved for a second until he made out the rest of her words. "Hector, the wall! You have to stop the giant!"

Hector's mind spun. He couldn't see. He couldn't breathe. Each rolling step threatened to break his hold on the slippery glass jar. But Amber's warning solidified in his mind. The giant had been facing the city wall. Now it lumbered forward. Amber must not be able to reach the levers that controlled the clockwork. Hector had to stop it.

Lightning crackled around him. He reached up to grab something to pull himself off the plate. A tendril of lightning connected with his flesh. He screamed and returned his hold to the glass. Somehow the glass and the ceramic kept him safe.

"Hector!" Amber yelled louder. "Stop it! Stop it!"

Hector gritted his teeth, choking on the stench of his burned hand. He'd been burned before. Nothing hurt so bad. Fear paralyzed him. He couldn't let go or the lightning would kill him. He had to stay on the plate.

A loud crash echoed through the giant as it hit the wall. Stone crumbled beneath the metal onslaught. Nothing could stop the giant, not walls or buildings or people. It could destroy the city and kill hundreds. He couldn't let that happen.

Crying out in despair, Hector reached up from the plate and pulled himself into the lightening-filled tangle of tubes and wires above him.

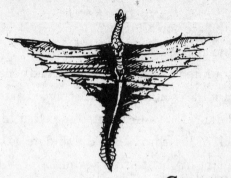

CHAPTER FOUR

The Bronze Giant stopped with one leg on the inside of the broken wall, the other leg on the outside. Its torso stood right in the middle. Amber sucked in a frightened breath, still clinging to the giant's open chest plate that swung back and forth, threatening to dislodge her. Fine sand billowed up from the last of the falling bricks, making her cough.

Humans raced at her along the unbroken portion of the wall. Those on the ground stepped out from where they'd fled as the giant lumbered toward them.

Now the giant stood still again, as if it had never been alive the moment before. The humans' angry voices rose above the sudden silence.

Frightened, Amber waited for the chest plate to swing close to the giant. Then she dived onto the clockwork inside. "Hector," she called. "Hector, we're in trouble. Come up here."

She strained to hear an answer, but only silence and the smell of burned flesh greeted her.

"Hector, are you all right?"

Still no answer.

She squinted to see where Hector had gone inside the massive giant. He should never have crawled in there. Crazy. Crazy and dangerous. She wanted to yell at him, but the words stuck in her throat. She didn't dare go down after him. The giant might start up again.

One of the tubes wiggled, and a blackened hand appeared, gripping it, followed by another that was not quite so burned. Then Hector's bald head rose out of the giant. Burns covered one side. He looked up at Amber with bloodshot eyes.

"Help me." His plea came out in a choking rasp.

Amber leaned over, got her hands under his shoulders, and pulled. Hector groaned in pain, but she got him up to the opening and propped him against the giant's clockwork.

Hector coughed and coughed until blood came up.

"We have to get down, but we don't have any ropes or pulleys," Amber muttered in distress.

"Hey!" Shem's angry voice sounded from the wall.

Amber twisted around to see him a few yards away, standing on the edge of the wall, glaring at the broken section before him. Wind whipped his loose-fitting clothes. Shock spread across his weathered face.

"Look what you did!" he cried. "We just rebuilt this wall, and you promised you could control the giant."

"Hector's hurt bad!" Amber yelled back. Never mind about the stupid wall. Hector had risked his life trying to make the giant work for her. Deep regret for her outburst in the night filled her. She'd pushed him to this. "Shem, he needs a healer. Please, help." Amber eased down beside Hector and wrapped her arm around his burned shoulders. He cried out in pain.

Shem got hold of a wooden plank and laid it across the gap between the giant's open chest and the wall. He crossed the plank in two long strides and lifted Hector in his arms. "I was afraid something like this might happen. The giant is just too dangerous. I forbid either of you to ever go near it again."

Amber's heart sank. They had made it work. Somehow Hector had done it. He could tell her how. They could make it safe. They could invent a way to control it.

She followed Shem as he carried Hector across the plank to the unbroken part of the wall. Shem lowered him to the stone. Hector closed his eyes. His breath came in painful rasps.

"Someone get a healer up here," Shem ordered. "You listen to me, Hector. If you touch this monstrosity again, I'll lock you up for the rest of your life." He took off his silk shirt, tore it into strips, and wrapped them around Hector's burns. "I mean it—for your own safety as well as everyone else's."

Hector wiped a dribble of blood from his chin and nodded. "The rest of my life might not be very long."

"No," Amber wailed. "You'll be all right. You have to be. Now you know how the giant works, we can go build our own giant back in Haggersmoore. Our people understand when things go wrong. You can't have great inventions without"—she stared at the broken wall—"some mishaps."

Hector's lips twisted into a smile. "I think I've figured it out, the perfect communication device." He coughed again and fell unconscious.

With his left hand, Hector set the small copper disk on the work table. His right hand throbbed beneath the bandages. The lightning burns on the side of his head and down his shoulders and back had also been bandaged. Those burns hurt almost as much as his lungs, which had been damaged by the fumes from the acid. Yet he'd refused the herbs that would have kept him in painless sleep.

"Lightning," he muttered in excitement as he placed a circular piece of blotting paper over the copper disk and covered it with a piece of zinc. A shiver of excitement went through him, pushing away the pain.

Amber hovered close by. "You should be resting. Save

that for later. You've got to recover so we can get back to Haggersmoore."

Hector grimaced. Living with other gnomes wasn't so bad, and he did sort of miss his father. But not now, not when he finally had an idea worth pursuing. Not now that the giant had shown him how to make lightning.

"Imagine," Hector said, "if we could send a message as fast as lightning. Think what the world would be like. No more wars. No more misunderstanding. Everyone could share all their knowledge with everyone else. Evil wouldn't have a chance to flourish in some hidden corner." Hector kept talking while he continued to stack his lightning cylinder. Amber kept up a dialogue of her own.

"We can go to Haggersmoore and build our own giant," she said. "Now we know how to generate that much power we can make any invention we want, however big we want. I bet I could make a mechanical dog or bear. I could build a machine big enough to move an entire house all at once. We'll have a whole army of mechanical warriors." She sat down and started scribbling away, sketching her mechanical wonders.

Ignoring her, Hector threaded two wires through the discs to fasten his cylinder together and dipped it in a mixture of vinegar and salt—a safe acid to start with. He'd been burned enough, and the fumes from the acid in the giant had made his lungs feel like they'd been shredded by a lion.

Gingerly he grabbed one end of the wires. A small shock went through him. He laughed and touched the wires again. Another shock. He'd done it, made his own lightning.

"Just call me a blue dragon," he crowed, then chuckled at the thought of a cylinder like his resting inside a blue dragon's belly.

CHAPTER FIVE

Kyani poked his nose up through the sand and sniffed. Scorching heat filled the air with the scent of rocks and sand and sage. Still sniffing, he pushed his head up farther out of the bolt-hole and scanned the sky for the blue dragon that had almost killed him the last time he ventured out of the lair. If he'd been a second slower, he might have died just like his parents. But his parents had not tried to escape—they'd gone out to fight the blue dragon and lost.

Their sacrifice had given Kyani a chance to live.

"But I can't stay hidden in the lair forever," Kyani muttered. The sun warmed his faceplates, inviting him to come out. The sky stretched overhead in a cloudless, empty expanse. No sign of the blue dragon.

Kyani swept out of the hole, sand shivering down his scales to the ground. He rippled his wings, and more sand scurried away to join with the rest of the desert. He'd chosen an exit on the north side, well away from the west

31

where his parents had fallen. It seemed safer. The blue dragon had appeared so quickly last time, it had to have been watching from some high perch on one of the desert's many stone pinnacles.

Kyani stretched and shuffled forward, kicking a group of pebbles in front of him. "Little pebbles," he said, "aren't you the lucky ones? You get to stay out here all the time. No worries about blue dragons. No one wants to bother you, except me."

He laughed and picked one up with his long tongue. The stone tasted like clay with a faint bit of iron. He spit it out, arranged it into a circle with the other pebbles, and danced around on top of them.

A black beetle, dislodged by his rumpus, scurried away.

Kyani sniffed at it until it disappeared beneath a larger rock. "Hey, come back here, Blackie. I won't step on you."

The beetle remained hidden.

Kyani circled the rock. "Come out and talk to me." The beetle refused to come out. Kyani grabbed the rock and lifted it. No beetle. Just a hole in the ground that the beetle had escaped into. Kyani sniffed and dropped the rock.

Keeping his eyes out for the blue dragon, Kyani ambled away from the rock formations that marked his lair. The vast, empty desert stretched out in front of him. Only tall cacti broke the endless flat. Sagebrush and tumbleweed rustled as he slid through them. The dunes glittered beyond the cacti. Nothing grew out there.

A wren chattered at Kyani from the arm of a cactus. Kyani greeted the bird, but it zipped into the air and sped away. On the ground, a long copper snake with a diamond pattern on its back lounged in the sun.

"You there," Kyani said. "Have you seen the blue dragon?" The snake slithered away and vanished into the sand.

"Fine. Go back to your lair," Kyani said, walking away. "But I'm not going back to mine until I find someone to talk to. I can't stand being alone anymore."

Hector smiled at the group of humans gathered in the front entry of Shem's massive bronze palace. They were dressed in the loose-fitting brown and tan robes typical of desert people. Shem stood in front of the group, watching Hector fondly. "I'm glad to see you've been working on something else instead of worrying about the giant."

Hector rubbed his hands together. "You're really going to like this."

Shem's half-elf daughter, Shara, smiled at Hector and waited, graceful and patient—more patient than Peyote, the captain of the city guard, who held his spear in one hand

and had his scimitar strapped to his waist. He fidgeted, making it clear he had far better things to do than stand around and listen to Hector.

The gnome ignored him. It didn't matter what Peyote thought. He needed to impress Shem and no one else. His demonstration should do it. His invention had come a long way while he healed from his burns.

"Distinguished leaders of Kaal," Hector said, rolling his device out into the center of the room. "I have brought a most wondrous thing to show you."

He launched into a detailed explanation about how he'd made his own lightning in a cylinder, and how he could send the lightning where he wanted along a wire, and how by controlling the pulses he could send messages in the blink of an eye. Of course there had to be a way to receive the messages at the end of the wire, which is what his demonstration would show.

Peyote stepped forward and waved his hand. "Stop jabbering nonsense and show us what this does."

"Right." Hector pulled a lever that lowered his row of connected cylinders into the acid. Lightning raced up his wire to where he had it wound around an iron core, then back down again to his cylinders.

"Now watch this," Hector said. He set a large piece of iron beneath his coiled wire. The power from the lightning going through the coil lifted the heavy iron off the ground as if by magic and held it in place against the core. "You see," Hector said, "that's how the Bronze Giant moves."

Shem gave him a warning look.

"But I'm not going anywhere near the giant. This is for something different—something much better. You see, the lightning in the wire has the power to move objects at the other end. So we just have to hook up a writing device, and we can use this to send messages to Purespring, or even to the dwarf kingdom clear across the desert to the mountains on the other side."

Laughter exploded from the humans, filling the hall.

Shem shook his head. "Hector, this is the craziest thing you've come up with yet." He reached over to Hector's lightning machine.

"No!" Hector cried. Too late. Shem's hand closed around the copper wire, and the lightning flashed through him down to the ground.

Hector leaped to the lever and pulled it, shutting off the lightning.

Shem fell to the floor, his hand blackened. His hair stood straight up on his head, and his face leeched of all color. The piece of iron clattered down beside him. Hector rushed over, but the humans pushed him away.

"Is he dead?" someone asked.

"No. His heart's beating, faintly. I think he's still breathing."

Hector let out a sigh of relief. While the humans fussed over Shem, he wheeled his invention to the door. He'd have to come up with some way to make it safe.

"Hector!" Shem's angry voice boomed across the hall. Hector froze.

"I want you and your crazy inventions out of my city."

Hector turned back to face Shem. Shem stood, his face no longer white, but livid red. He pointed at Hector with his burned hand. "You are a menace. Get that thing out of here. Get out and never come back."

Hector's heart sank. Humans just didn't understand. If Shem would have listened to him while he explained about the lightning, none of this would have happened.

"But I've already set up the sender-receiver device," Hector protested. "Just give me a chance. I'll show you that it works. I'll make it safe. I promise."

Tight lipped, Shem jabbed his finger at the door.

Hector trundled his device outside where Amber stood waiting. The sun glinted off her tawny hair. The gold bracelet around her wrist jangled as she waved to the humans inside.

The door slammed shut behind Hector.

"Don't worry about them," Amber said, patting him on the back. "Humans only understand simple devices. Why, when I helped some of them escape from the slave mines, all they wanted me to make was stone knives for them. Imagine. Out of all my inventions, they just wanted that." She shook her head. "Humans just don't get it."

Hector pushed his cart down the street to the lab. Amber was right, but there had been one human once who understood him: His friend Mudd would have listened about the lightning machine and been excited.

Back inside, Hector hooked his invention up to the sender-receiver device. The coiled wire sat above an arm that held a stick of charcoal over a long strip of paper.

"I guess that's it," Amber said. "We better pack up. I told you we should go to Haggersmoore. We'll take your machines with us and use it to power my inventions. It will be wonderful." She raced around, packing up the lab.

Hector rubbed his twice-burned bald head. "There has to be a way to show them, to convince them my invention works."

"They won't let you do it, Hector." Amber's bracelet jangled, and she whistled as she packed up her things.

Hector's head pounded, and he longed for a cool drink of water to quench his thirst and clear his thoughts.

"Come on." Amber grabbed his hand and tugged him toward his room. "I'll help you pack."

"No. Leave me alone." He pulled away from her. "And stop all that infernal noise. I'm trying to think." Hector picked up a coil of copper wire from the worktable. "The lightning doesn't like glass or ceramic. There must be some other substances it doesn't like, something I can coat the wire with to make it safe. Let's see." He scribbled a list of things to try: cotton, beeswax, flax . . .

Amber stood for a long moment where he'd left her. "I'm going to Haggersmoore," she said, her face wrinkling up as if she might cry. "Are you coming with me?"

"No," Hector said, distracted by his list. "I'm going to prove to them this invention works, whatever it takes."

"But you can't stay here. Shem just kicked us out."

"You're right, I can't stay here, but they'll never notice if I leave one of the sender-receivers behind. I can coat the wires tonight and bury a line going out of the city. Then in the morning I'll pack everything up and head out. I'll string a line straight across the desert to the dwarf kingdom and set up another sender-receiver. Then I'll have that dwarf prince, Goldmane, send a message across it to Shem. That will show him. That will prove how useful my device is."

Amber shook her head. "You don't have to prove anything to Shem. You've done all this work to help him, and he doesn't want it. But I do. I want your help, Hector. Please come with me."

"I've got it!" Hector cried. "The perfect coating, and I have the supplies here to make it." Forgetting Amber, he rushed to the supply closet.

Amber raced after him and caught his arm. "Hector, stop."

"What? What's wrong?" Hector said, wrenching his arm away and opening the closet.

"You're what's wrong," Amber cried. "You never listen to what I'm saying. You don't try to understand what's really important to me. All you're thinking about is yourself."

"That's not true!" Hector yelled. "I'm not thinking about myself at all. I'm thinking about an invention that will help the whole world."

CHAPTER SIX

ector carried the last armload of equipment out to the wagon in front of the lab. Morning sun glared down at him, already sending ripples of heat up from the ground. Thistle, who was hitched to the cart, let out a plaintive bray.

"Be patient one more minute, Thistle," he said, patting the donkey's gray back. "We're going soon."

He returned to the lab and took a deep breath. Amber hovered just inside the door, staring at him without saying anything. There wasn't much left to say. They'd both shouted themselves hoarse the night before while Hector worked. Amber would not budge, and he would not change his mind. This invention was too important.

"Come out into the desert with me," Hector pleaded one last time. "Help me set up the device." He took her calloused hand. Her bracelet jangled close to his fingertips.

She pulled away. "Good-bye, Hector." She walked out of the lab and headed up the street to the city gate where a large caravan of traders was getting ready to head to Purespring, the first stop on the road that would take Amber home. Her small body disappeared among the tall humans.

The morning suddenly felt chilly. Hector frowned and rubbed his head. "The greatest invention in all of history, and she walks away?"

Hector stepped back into the empty room. He stared at the worktable that was scarred black here and there from various experiments, the swept floor, the broom leaning against the cupboard where Amber had left it, and the bare hooks on the wall where they had hung their aprons. A lone pair of wire cutters lay on the table. Hector picked them up. The black leather grips fit his hands perfectly from years of use. He shoved the cutters into his apron pocket.

The only sign of life left in the room huddled in one corner—Hector's sender-receiver device with its row of lightning cylinders and the coiled wire that worked the writing arm. Its twin was already waiting in the back of the wagon for Hector to take it to the dwarf kingdom.

He crossed the room, pulling a small book out of his pocket. He set it down on the machine next to the writing arm and opened it to show the cipher that would turn the dots and dashes from the sender-receiver into words.

"There, Master Shem," he said. "When I'm done, you'll get Goldmane's message. You'll thank me for this in the end." He pulled an oil cloth over the contraption to hide it from unwanted attention.

Peyote stepped into the room with a stern look on his face. "Master Shem sent me to escort you out of the city."

"Right." Hector nodded. Keeping his eyes away from the sender-receiver in the back corner, Hector marched out of the room. Excitement filled him. Now, more than any time in his life, he knew what mattered most and how he could accomplish it.

He went to the cart and slapped the reins across Thistle's back.

The Bronze Giant's towering form loomed over him as he approached the city wall. The citizens had already rebuilt the breach, cementing the stones right up against the giant where it stood one foot inside the city, one foot outside, its back to the desert and its metal face looking over the city like some benevolent god.

Hector waved to the giant. "Thank you," he whispered, "for giving me your secret."

By the time he reached the gate, the caravan had already set out. The sand billowed up in a cloud from the horses and wagons. Though he strained, he couldn't see Amber.

Peyote reached over and caught Hector's arm as soon as they were outside the gate. Even on the wagon seat, Hector was barely the same height as the man.

"Master Shem says to tell you he's sorry for yelling. And sorry that he has to send you away. He likes you, but your inventions are too dangerous."

Hector nodded. "I understand." He reached into his apron and pulled out a sealed letter addressed to Shem. On the front, Hector had added a note that read, "Open in three weeks."

Peyote took it. Hector waved good-bye as he pretended to follow the caravan. But as soon as Peyote was gone, he turned his donkey back to the open desert. Within the hour he'd found the spot at the back wall where his wire came up from the ceramic pipe he'd laid it in underground.

The sun beat down on his bald head, and Hector lifted a hood up over it to keep it from burning. Then he took the end of the long copper wire he had coiled in the wagon and spliced it into the wire he'd laid from his lab. Sweat soaked his clothes as he worked, and he glanced up often to the top of the wall, hoping no one came along and saw him.

The splice was easy. The next part took a lot of work. Hector got out a pick and dug a posthole, then slid a wooden pole out of the wagon and into the ground. As soon as he had it secure, he strung the wire up the post and wrapped it around a glass knob affixed to the pole.

Something moved on top of the wall. Hector froze, one hand on the pole, the other on the wire.

"Hey you, what are you doing down there?" a voice called.

"Just leaving." Hector waved and went back to his cart. He urged the donkey forward. As he went, the copper wire uncoiled and slipped inch by inch out of the back of the wagon.

The person on the wall vanished.

Hector stopped Thistle and wiped the sweat from his forehead. Cracked white clay lay beneath his wheels. Scraggly gray plants fought to grow here and there around a cluster of tall cacti. "Welcome to the desert," he said to Thistle. "We're going to have a long trip."

He climbed into the back of the wagon and dipped a tin cup into the water barrel secured to one side. The warm water tasted stale but moistened his dry throat. He gave some to Thistle, who sucked it up and then shook his head, sending flecks of foamy water onto Hector's face.

Hector laughed, got out a ladder, set it up next to the tallest cactus, and climbed up. He pulled a glass knob out of his apron and secured it to the top. Then he lifted the wire that had lain across the ground. It rose into the air, stretching in a long arc between the cactus and the post. He fixed it to the knob, then climbed down and loaded up the ladder.

"One section up. One hundred miles to go." The glaring sun and stifling heat couldn't keep him from smiling. "You see, Amber. I'm brilliant." He turned to give her a hug like he'd done so many times back in the lab—only she wasn't there. A twinge of regret passed through him.

"At least you're here," he said to Thistle as he climbed back onto the wagon and headed for another tall cactus in the distance.

Hector gave Thistle another drink of water, then squinted back the way he'd come. He'd made slow progress, and the glaring sun made it difficult to see the gentle sweep of his wire.

He slumped against the side of the wagon. "Too hot," he muttered.

Sand whispered around him, finding its way into his clothes and chafing his skin. He knew he should pull the ladder out one more time, but his vision swam. Thistle brayed as if to say they'd only been out here for three quarters of a day. He should be stronger. This couldn't be so hard.

"I just need to rest," he told the donkey. "You do too."

He unhooked Thistle from the wagon and led him around to the shady side. The sun had already started for the far horizon, but that did not relieve the heat. Thistle rolled to the ground, taking up most of the shade.

Hector rubbed his head. "We can't go on this way." He sat down next to the donkey, leaned against the wagon wheel, and closed his eyes. The next thing he knew, the sun had vanished and the desert lay in darkness.

With the heat gone, Hector's head cleared. He got up and took a drink, then offered hay and water to Thistle. Stars glimmered in the sky. Solinari, the silver moon, smiled down on him, lighting the cacti and eddies of sand.

"Of course," Hector said, rubbing his hands together in excitement. "We'll work at night when it's cool, and rest during the day. How does that sound?"

Thistle blinked at him and walked to the front of the wagon so Hector could hitch him up.

CHAPTER SEVEN

Hector stopped the wagon and carried his ladder over to the last tall cactus before the shifting dunes that spread out ahead of him. The night breeze rustled across the sand. Thistle cocked an ear and then brayed in fright as if the sand had whispered a warning.

"Easy there. It's just the wind," Hector said.

Thistle tugged against his harness and brayed again.

Hector tensed. Thistle had been quiet and steady most of their trip. Strange that he should act up now. Hector looked around for any sign of danger, but saw none. The desert smelled like heated rocks and something else that might have been rotting flesh. Hector wrinkled his nose and tightened his grip on the smooth wooden ladder. A lot of things died out here in the desert. It was probably an old snake or something.

Swallowing to wet his dry throat, Hector tried to set the ladder up amid a scattering of boulders that surrounded the last cactus.

Even working at night, he hadn't made much progress over the past week. Out in the sand, he knew it would take him even longer. With no more cacti to use, he'd have to dig holes to erect his posts. Maybe that's what bothered Thistle. They'd already used up more than half their food and water. The dunes stretched out in vast waves with rocky spires barely visible on the far side.

Hector gritted his teeth and thumped the ladder down between two rocks. Something soft gave way beneath it, and he heard a skittering sound. Thistle filled the air with a terrified cry and kicked at the wagon, trying to free himself.

Hector scanned the ground for a snake, but saw no movement. Starlight illuminated the tops of the rocks with a faint silvery light. The bottom sides lay in darkness. Nothing moved beneath.

"Shhh, Thistle. Please, everything is fine. Just let me get this last section up, then we'll move on." Amid the donkey's continued braying, Hector climbed the ladder and fastened the glass knob to the cactus. Then he climbed back down to grab the copper wire.

Out of the corner of his eye, Hector saw a shadow move by the wagon. He turned, startled. His breath caught in his throat. He strained to see anything out of place in the blackness below the wagon. Nothing moved.

"Dumb donkey, now you have me seeing things." He grabbed the wire and climbed back up the ladder. His hands shook as he secured the wire around the knob. The desert wind whipped across the sand, giving him goose bumps.

Licking his cracked lips, he moved down the ladder, searching the ground for any sign of the movement he'd seen before. His foot crunched onto the rocky ground. He tucked the ladder under his arm and walked to the wagon. As he neared the back, a long, thin shadow detached itself from a rock and sped at him.

Hector froze.

If he made no sudden movements, the snake would leave him alone. Except the creature kept coming, across his foot, onto his boot. It couldn't be a snake. It had close to a hundred legs, which it used to propel itself up Hector.

Hector yelped, dropped the ladder, and batted at the giant centipede. Before he could get it off, it sank its fangs through his trousers and into his skin.

He batted at it again, this time succeeding in sending it flying. It crunched against a rock a few feet away. As soon as it hit the ground, it turned around and came back at him.

Hector raced toward the front of the wagon, but the leg the centipede had bitten gave out beneath him. He realized with growing terror that the poison had paralyzed his right leg.

Gotta get out of here, Hector thought. Get on the wagon and go.

He staggered, glancing behind him as the centipede rushed after him.

A sharp pain pricked just below his left knee. He turned to see a second centipede already on him. He flung it off, but the poison spread through both of his legs. Too late to run. He'd have to fight them.

He jerked a wrench from his apron and swung it at the closest one. The creature made a sickening crunch beneath the metal and slumped, dead.

The second centipede darted forward and tried to bite his hand before he lifted it back up. Hector changed the direction of his movement and caught the creature in the middle, flinging it back several feet.

An awful smell filled the air from the dead centipede, but it seemed to just drive the second one into a frenzy. It scuttled forward, biting rocks, biting the ground, biting its fallen friend.

Hector let out a breath. Perhaps it would be content feasting on its smashed companion. Fighting against the paralyzing poison, Hector forced himself to the side of the wagon, then realized he'd left his ladder where he'd dropped it. Without the ladder he'd never get the wire strung across the desert.

"Don't be stupid. You can make a new one," he told himself while watching the frenzied centipede writhe on top of the dead one. "Just get on the wagon and go."

He caught the side of the wagon and tried to draw himself up onto the seat. Almost faster than he could see them, two more centipedes climbed up the wheel and onto his chest.

He screamed and tore them off.

A dozen more shadows moved on the ground, racing at him.

Thistle's brays turned to deafening screams as the whole clutch of centipedes converged on the donkey and Hector.

The creatures reached Hector and swarmed all over his body, biting him, biting one another, biting themselves. Stabbing pain prickled Hector's skin everywhere, then the poison numbed him and he fell, unable to feel the creatures, unable to move to get away.

CHAPTER EIGHT

Amber swayed back and forth with the rhythm of the wagon as it sighed over the drifting sand. Foss, the wagon driver, clucked to his horses, urging them to keep up with the rest of the caravan that stretched out in front of them. The lead wagons were no more than blocky shadows that moved across the desert in the cool of the late night. In another hour or two, the light of dawn would peek over the dunes in the distant east.

Amber kept her hands in her pockets, fingering the tools she most often kept there—a screwdriver or two, a couple of wrenches, everyday items that a person could not live without. In her mind she created the blueprints she would need to build her own Bronze Giant.

Now that she knew the secret to capturing and using lightning, she could power any creation she wanted. She didn't need Hector with her, so why did her heart hurt so much? She felt like someone had torn out the clockwork mechanism that kept her running—not that gnomes ran on clockwork. Something just felt broken inside her when she thought of Hector. She pictured him happily stringing his wire across the desert and wondered what the odds were that his sender-receiver device would work at the distance he was trying to attain.

She shook her head, and her hair fluttered in her face. When she reached up to brush it aside, her bracelet jangled. That sound used to make her happy.

"Stupid Hector," she muttered. Why stay here and try to impress the humans? Better to go home.

She thought of her home in Haggersmoore, with its waterwheel to power the cogs and gizmos, its long work-benches, the upper-downer system that could carry her from the basement to the fifth floor in the blink of an eye. It usually worked too, and when it didn't she had a pool of water below to break her fall.

She stared around at the vast, empty desert and shuddered at the silence. In Haggersmoore there was always the ping of hammers and the squeal of gears, shouts and thumps and bangs. She'd been gone too long.

What had been a simple trip to the Vingaard Mountains to collect some minerals for one of her inventions had ended with her being captured by the durogar dwarves and forced to work in their mines. That hadn't been too bad. She'd been able to invent a useful rock mover and other things. But the human slaves she worked with had suffered terribly at the hands of the dwarves.

She'd helped the humans escape in the end. After which she'd seen the Bronze Giant, and that was something she'd never forget. Such an interesting creation. And they'd learned so much from it, she and Hector . . . Hector. Her eyes stung, and she rubbed at them, furious with herself. He'd been away from home as long as she had. He should want to go back with her.

"You all right?" Foss asked. He'd been kind enough to let her ride with him across the desert. She didn't have the steel to pay him, but she'd kept his wagon working well even when others broke down from sand in the axles. He said that service was better than steel.

Amber took a deep breath. It caught in her throat so she had a hard time answering that she was fine.

Foss unwound the brown scarf that kept the sand out of his face, took a drink of water, and offered some to Amber. She thanked him and sucked up a dainty gulp of the stale, hot liquid.

"I'll just be glad when we're out of the desert," she said.

"I know what you mean," Foss answered. "If I didn't make so much steel selling my herbs in Kaal I'd never set foot in the desert again."

Amber smiled at the thought of never returning to the desert. But Hector was out there somewhere in the vast emptiness. She hoped he would be all right.

"Look there," Foss said. He pointed ahead of them. A cluster of black mounds appeared on the horizon. As they drew closer, Amber realized they were adobe houses. A large domed building graced the center of the cluster.

"Purespring," Foss said. "Our first step on the road back to green lands."

Hector lay on the ground, unable to move while the swarm of centipedes crawled over his chest and legs, biting him and fighting with one another. The rustle of their bodies filled the air with a terrifying cacophony.

He could not feel their many legs against his skin or their numerous bites and stings. He could smell them though, the sickening stench of rancid meat. Bile rose in his throat as he realized he would die here, eaten alive. His initial screams had long since ceased, his throat too dry and ragged to make any more sound.

Overhead the stars looked down on him, cold and unfeeling. They had no care for a single gnome in the vast desert. Hector imagined the gods laughing at him. Their laughs turned quickly to accusation in his mind. We control lightning. Who do you think you are, to try and capture the power of the gods? Did you think we would let you create a device that could change our world? You are nothing but dust. Food for worms.

Hector managed a rasping laugh. Not worms. Centipedes. The creatures swarmed over him in a relentless feeding frenzy. Hector leaned back and closed his eyes. He couldn't watch anymore. Let me die quickly, he thought.

The sound of rushing wind covered him. Sand whipped against his face.

"Hey," a deep voice boomed out. "What's going on? You critters having a party without me?"

Something heavy thumped to the sand, making the ground tremble.

Hector snapped his eyes open and saw a huge, winged form leaning over him. In the dark of night it made a menacing black shape against the sky. After a moment, he realized it was a dragon.

"Help." Hector managed a dry squeak, but he doubted anyone would save him from the dragon anymore than anyone would from the centipedes.

"Wow," the dragon said. "I didn't know centipedes could talk. At least none have talked to me yet. Which of you said that?"

Hector gulped, trying to get enough moisture in his throat to speak, though why he bothered at that point he wasn't sure. Getting eaten by centipedes was bad enough without adding a dragon into the mix. "I'm not a centipede," he tried to shout, but it came out more of a whisper. "I'm a gnome. The centipedes are eating me, so if you want me for dinner you'll have to get rid of them first."

The dragon's plated face leaned down for a closer look. He stared at the writhing mass for a moment, then reached out with one claw and brushed the centipedes aside.

"What's a gnome?" he said. "I've never seen or smelled anything like you before."

The centipedes raced back to Hector.

"I'm a gnome," Hector cried. "And I'd rather be eaten by you than by them."

The dragon swatted the centipedes away again. "Why would I want to eat you? I'd much rather talk to you. I can eat anything, but you're the first creature that has talked back to me since—" He broke off and looked away.

The centipedes took advantage of that to swarm all over Hector again.

Hector screamed, surprised that he had any juice left to do that.

The dragon swung his head back and glared at the centipedes. "Annoying little monsters," he said. "Enough of that." He sucked in a breath and then let loose a cloud of billowing gas.

It settled over Hector and the centipedes, smelling like hot metal. Exhaustion soaked through him, and he blinked. So tired. All around and on top of him the centipedes flopped down and stopped moving.

The dragon reached for him, and Hector closed his eyes. He was barely aware as the dragon lifted him into the air and carried him away.

Chapter Nine

Kyani flapped his wings, lifting the small talking creature into the air with him. He regretted having to use his sleep gas. It seemed the only way to stop the centipedes from interrupting his conversation. Of course it put the gnome to sleep too, which ended the conversation just the same. Of all the bother.

He kept his eyes open for the hated blue dragon as he flew across the desert. There had been no sign of it since the attack just after his parents' death. Perhaps the Blue felt Kyani was too small to be worth the trouble. Or better yet, the blue dragon thought he'd killed Kyani when Kyani had escaped into the bolt-hole just as the last bit of lightning burned the sand behind him.

Feeling warm and satisfied, Kyani flew toward the rock formations that marked his lair. The gnome rested lightly in his front claws. Blood dripped from hundreds of bites on its body. The scent of it stung Kyani's nose. He sneezed and shook his head.

Rocks and sand and cacti passed below him as he retraced the path he'd taken from the lair. Well, not exactly "retraced." When he'd left home, he'd wandered here and there, sometimes in circles, sometimes in lines, going from one plant to the next, watching for any movement on the sand. He'd talked to three snakes, ten scorpions, some ground squirrels, and several birds, but none of them talked back.

Now Kyani flew in a straight line. The gnome was hurt, and the smell of blood was likely to bring all kinds of trouble.

The towering rocks took shape ahead of him, bathed in faint pink light from the coming sun. In the center tower, a cave mouth opened, with a little hidden path and steps carved into the stone. Kyani veered away from it. The lair's front entry led into a maze of tunnels that went nowhere. A second false entry lay on the east side of the rock formation, facing the rising sun.

Kyani tucked the gnome to his chest to shield him and dived into a sand-filled bolt-hole out on the desert floor. The golden sand slid across Kyani's scales in a familiar caress, and then he was home, back in the tunnels that still smelled faintly like his parents. Back where he used to talk with them all day and long into the nights. He still ached when he thought of his parents' death. He couldn't stand the lair's endless silence without them.

Carrying the gnome, he hurried through the long maze of tunnels, past the Grand Conversation Hall to a resting chamber beyond.

The cool chamber had a smooth rock in the center for sleeping on and a pool of clear water against the far wall for bathing and drinking.

The best part of the room was the large fireplace on one side, where Kyani could lie and watch the flames for hours on end. He breathed a puff of fire at the dead sage and twisted desert wood that waited on the hearth. The wood caught fire and its flames lit the chamber.

Kyani lay the gnome on the rock, then went to the pool and scooped up some water to wash away the blood. He dumped it on the creature, and rivulets of pink slid across the rock as the blood washed away. But more blood welled up from the wounds. Kyani shook his head in frustration. He knew nothing of healing. He tried more water, with the same result.

The shock of the cold water woke the gnome. Its eyes fluttered open, but it lay limp and unmoving on the rock.

"Am I dead yet?" the gnome asked.

"No, of course not," Kyani said. But he worried. With all the blood loss, the gnome could die.

"Are you going to eat me now or later?" The gnome's voice cracked, and he seemed almost too weak to talk.

"Neither. I don't want to eat you. I just want to talk to you." Kyani leaned over to give the gnome a friendly lick on the face.

The gnome's eyes widened. "I don't think I'll be much good for talking if I don't get these wounds bandaged soon. I'm a bit paralyzed at the moment. Do you think you could do it?"

"Bandaged?" Kyani let the unfamiliar word roll around his mouth. "Bandaged. Bandaged. Bandaged, bandaged. Hey, I like that word. What does it mean?"

The gnome choked. "You get material and wrap it tight around the wounds to stop the bleeding. Do you have any cotton or linen fabric?"

"Oh sure. We have all different kinds of fabrics here." Kyani left the gnome and hurried down the tunnel and across the Grand Conversation Hall to the Hall of Art.

"Let's see now, what will make the best bandage?" There was the blue shimmery material he'd tried to talk to earlier. A rack on the wall down a little farther held a gold fabric that looked like dragon scales. Beside that was a bolt of red velvet. Then a rainbow of shimmering silks.

He sniffed at each type of material. The gnome had asked for cotton or linen. Those were common fabrics, and his parents might not have bothered to collect them. He sniffed a bolt of fabric as green as the trees in the big tapestry. It smelled like animal hair, sheep wool probably.

It would have to do. Grabbing it, he ran back to the resting chamber.

The gnome's eyes had closed again.

Kyani spread out the fabric and laid it on top of him. "How's that?" Kyani asked. "Will you live now? Can you talk to me?"

The gnome groaned and opened his eyes. It took him a moment to focus on Kyani and another moment to speak. "You must tear the fabric in strips and tie them tight around my wounds. Then could you please get me a drink of water?"

"Of course. Of course." Kyani snatched up the material and tore it into strips. In the back of his mind he could hear his father scolding him for ruining the treasure. Kyani shook his head. His father would not come back to scold him. Better to use the fabric to save the gnome. Then he'd have someone to talk to again. The gnome had most likely been all over the world and could tell him many stories about all kinds of wonderful things.

The chamber echoed with the sound of the tearing fabric. That part was easy. Wrapping up the gnome's wounds was harder, but Kyani managed it.

He paused when he'd finished and looked over his clumsy handiwork. Most of the gnome's body was covered in bandages. Only his face and head had been spared from the centipedes.

"Water," the gnome croaked.

"Oh yes." Kyani went to the pool and scooped some up in his claw, but when he offered it to the gnome, he only succeeded in sloshing it across the gnome's face, almost drowning him.

The gnome sputtered, trying to catch his breath.

"Sorry about that," Kyani said.

The gnome gave him a limp smile. "Thanks for helping me."

"My pleasure." Kyani ruffled his wings and then folded them against his back and hunched down beside the gnome. "Do you think you'll be all right now?"

"Sure. Until the poison wears off and I start feeling all these bites. That's going to hurt."

"Don't worry. I'll stay with you," Kyani said. "My name's Tumbleweed, by the way. I'm a brass dragon." He knew better than to tell any creature his true name, and Tumbleweed was the nickname his father had often called him. He settled in for a long conversation with the gnome, but the gnome's eyes closed again before he'd gotten far in explaining about his parents and the blue dragon.

Kyani sighed and went to look for a bowl or goblet or something to give the gnome some water with when he woke up. They'd have plenty of time to talk after that.

"I'll never be alone again," Kyani whispered to himself, smiling.

Amber climbed down from the wagon at the edge of Purespring and waved good-bye to Foss. He clicked to his horses, urging them on to the stable yard that housed the teams and wagons for visiting merchants and people who'd come seeking the healing waters at the Wellspring Temple.

The morning sun already heated the sand-packed streets and rows of squat, mud-brick houses. Compared to Kaal's ancient splendor, Purespring was no more than a primitive village, but Amber had friends here, and that made it ten times better than Kaal.

Her stomach grumbled as the smell of morning biscuits filled the air. She waved as a human woman came out of her house and headed to the pools of fresh water to fill a pot for cooking.

The woman smiled and waved back.

"Good morning," the woman said.

"And you." Amber rubbed her apron and looked around. "Where's Syndall Goodlund's house?" Though Amber and Syndall had been through a lot together, this was Amber's first time in Purespring.

The woman laughed. "I figured you'd be looking for her. It's that big house there, on the far side of the village."

"Thanks," Amber said and raced away. Her bracelet jingled as she ran across town.

She passed the Wellspring Temple, with its beautiful dome and glittering stream of fresh water tumbling down from the pools inside. Nothing could be more precious in the desert than the sound of running water.

Amber knelt at the stream and quenched her thirst, then hurried across a little stone bridge to the other side and continued on to Syndall's house. It was a beautiful new two-story home, made of the same reddish adobe bricks as the other houses. Lace curtains fluttered in the house's windows, and the smell of sausages accompanied that of hot biscuits just out of the oven. Next to it stood a fabric shop where Syndall's parents worked their trade.

Amber trotted up to the heavy wooden door and knocked on it with a wrench from her apron pocket.

Syndall opened the door while rubbing the sleep from her grayish green eyes. Her short red hair stood up in a snarly mess. "Ah, Mother, it's too early," she said, blinking in the morning sun. "I'll come help you in the shop later."

"Sorry it's so early," Amber chirped. "I just got into town and figured I'd come find you. Didn't know you'd still be sleeping. Does that mean your father is doing the cooking?"

"Yes, he's cooking. Mother had to finish some important material today to trade with a merchant before he leaves town." Syndall blinked again and finally got her blurry eyes focused on Amber. She let out a yelp of surprise, flung the door open, and snatched Amber off the ground in a tight hug. "Amber, Amber! It's good to see you. I thought you'd be in Kaal forever. How are things going with the giant?"

Amber waited until Syndall stopped crushing the air out of her and put her down to speak. "Hector and I got the giant working. It crashed into the wall, and Shem kicked us out of the city. Well, he didn't kick us out until Hector nearly killed him with a lightning machine. Shem's nice enough, but that pushed him over the edge."

Syndall laughed. "Come on in and have breakfast with me."

Amber stepped into the cool entryway onto a blue and yellow rug, most certainly woven by Ariana, Syndall's mother. More of her brilliant work in the form of tapestries depicting a strong lady knight covered the walls.

Connal, Syndall's father, waved from the kitchen without looking up from the pan of sausages he attended. "Hello, Amber. Come in and get some breakfast."

Amber and Syndall stepped into the kitchen, but a high-pitched scream from the shop next door stopped them.

"Mother?" Syndall raced back out of the house with Connal and Amber right behind her.

Ariana appeared in the shop doorway, her face red and her hands shaking. "It's gone!" she cried. "The whole bolt of blue silk I spent the past two months making."

"Let me see," Connal said, stepping past her into the shop. "Maybe you just misplaced it."

Ariana slapped his shoulder as he passed. "You know I always put things away. It's gone, I tell you. Someone broke the lock on the shop door and stole it."

Amber stepped up to the door and examined the lock. "It's not actually broken," she said, fingering the exposed copper pieces. "It's just taken apart, rather expertly I might say."

Connal kicked the door in frustration. "We have to sell that today to get the money to keep the shop going."

"Come on," Syndall said, sprinting away down the street. "We'd better go tell the mayor. He'll help us find the thief."

Amber ran after her, forgetting about breakfast.

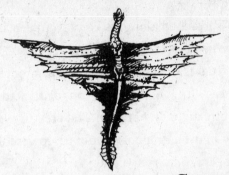

CHAPTER TEN

Hector woke with pain stabbing through his body. He screamed and sat up, fighting to tear the horrible centipedes from his chest and legs—only the creatures were already gone. Their numbing poison had worn off, and now he realized this pain was worse than when he couldn't feel at all. It made him yell and yell some more.

At the sound of his screams, a large shadow moved on the wall. With a jolt, Hector remembered he was no longer in the desert. A dragon had carried him into some kind of rocky lair.

Hector felt smooth sandstone beneath him. The ceiling of the dark chamber loomed above, lit by dancing flames. He turned his head to find the fire and saw the dragon sitting in front of a large fireplace. The dragon swung its gaze away from the flames and climbed to its feet.

In the firelight, Hector could tell it wasn't an evil dragon like he'd first thought out in the desert. Its scales glowed a burnished brass as it lumbered over to him. Its

69

wings were attached along its body from the shoulders to its tail, giving them the look of giant fans. A skull plate curved up from the dragon's cheeks into three sharp points above its head. Its long, pointed tongue flicked out.

Hector caught his breath. The creature, though not as big as he figured dragons should be, towered above him in shimmering majesty.

"You're awake," it said.

"I wish I weren't." Hector hardly dared speak.

The dragon's lips curled up into a smile, which amazed Hector. He'd never imagined a dragon could be so expressive. Then annoyance washed over him. "You don't have to be so happy," he said to the dragon. "I'm in pain here."

The dragon nodded. "I figured you would be. While you slept I had a long conversation with my father, and he suggested I give you some cactus juice. It will reduce the pain and help your wounds heal faster."

Hector had vague memories of the dragon talking to him before he fell unconscious. He could have sworn it had told him its name was Tumblebramble, or something like that, and both its parents were dead.

"Wasn't your father killed by a blue dragon?" Hector asked. Trying to think made his head throb along with the rest of him.

The dragon took a step back and shook himself. "You were awake? You heard me last night?"

Hector nodded—then wished he hadn't. He decided his best bet was to lie there and never move again.

"That's wonderful news!" The dragon danced around the room, furling and unfurling his glorious brass wings.

It reminded Hector of how young gnome children acted on completion of their earliest inventions. Then the truth dawned on him, and he knew why the dragon was so small. It was a young dragon, a child. An orphan.

A wave of sorrow washed over Hector, and he thought of his own father, Bloody Bob, back in Haggersmoore inventing weapons for the Solamnic Knights. Bloody Bob probably didn't even know Hector was still alive.

He frowned. "Listen, Tumblebumble, how did you talk to your father?" Hector wasn't sure he cared about that, but the thought of something to ease the intense pain from the centipede bites held his interest.

"Hey, my name's Tumbleweed. And talking to my father was easy. I just went into the Grand Conversation Hall, sat down, and told him everything about you and the centipedes." Sorrow filled the young dragon's eyes. "Of course he wasn't there to answer, so I had to sit and think and think and try to remember everything he'd ever told me about wounds. That's when I remembered about the cactus juice. While you were asleep I got you some."

Tumbleweed lifted a delicately carved wooden bowl from the floor and held it out to Hector.

Hector took it with shaking hands. Though it had looked small when the dragon held it, it was quite large to Hector. The bandages made it hard for him to hold it, but he lifted it to his lips and took a sip.

He'd gotten hurt enough times in the past to know how vile healing potions taste, so it surprised him to find the liquid cool and sweet. As soon as it touched his tongue it quenched his thirst. He gasped and took another sip. The liquid soothed his raw throat and its coolness spread out from his stomach, washing away the pain from his many bites.

The dragon eased the bowl out of his hands, and Hector realized he'd finished the whole drink.

"Better?" Tumbleweed asked.

"Yes. Much better." Hector lay back and stared at the red and orange walls above him. "Where are we? Where's my wagon and poor Thistle? He tried to warn me about the centipedes, but I just didn't understand what was spooking him so."

"I left your wagon out in the desert where I found you." Tumbleweed pointed vaguely behind him. "That other four-legged creature that was with you wasn't breathing. I think the biggest bunch of centipedes got to him first. You're lucky. If he hadn't been there you wouldn't have survived until I found you."

"No," Hector moaned. "I need Thistle to pull the wagon." Vast sands followed by the plains and Vingaard

River still stood between him and the Northern Dargaard Mountains. Without the donkey and wagon he'd never get the wire across to the dwarf kingdom.

The dragon ruffled his wings and edged closer to Hector. "Don't worry about the wagon. I can bring it here if you like. It will take quite some time for those wounds to heal."

Hector pictured the dragon lifting his wagon into the air, the copper wire, wooden posts, tools, and the second sender-receiver device sliding out the back as he flew, smashing to bits and scattering across the desert. And if the wire caught on the back of the wagon, the dragon could tear down the whole line he'd worked so hard to set up.

"No!" Hector cried. "Leave it alone. Just carry me back to it. I have important work to do."

The dragon's eyes narrowed. "You're in no condition to go back out into the desert."

"Yes I am. I'm fine." Hector leaped to his feet. A ringing sound filled his ears. Black spots appeared in front of his eyes, and the room spun.

The dragon caught him as he tumbled off the stone bed.

"Now there, you see?" Tumbleweed laid him back on the stone and pulled a shimmering blue material over him. "How's that? Do you like that? My father said that humans and other beings without scales like to have cloth over them to keep them warm while they sleep. I don't understand it. I think the desert is plenty warm. But then he also said it was important to keep injured people warm because their bodies go into shock and they could die. So there you are. My father's favorite piece of material. Now you'll be all comfortable. No big hurry to go anywhere. Just lie back and we'll have a nice long conversation. Don't you like to talk? I like to talk. You see, I've been terribly lonely since my parents were killed, and I've been looking for someone to talk to, and here you are, all hurt and needing time to recover, and here I am—I saved your life, you know—happy to sit here and keep you company."

Hector could hardly hear the dragon babble on through the ringing in his ears. He knew the dragon was right about one thing, though. He was in no condition to continue his work at the moment. He'd have to wait and recover. The thought of the wasted time chafed at him.

"So you see, I'm glad you're here. I'll feed you and tend your wounds and watch over you, and you can tell me all about the world beyond the desert." The dragon patted Hector's arm.

Hector closed his eyes. "There's not that much to tell."

"Of course there is. You can start by telling me why you don't have any hair. My father said that humans have hair. Of course you aren't human, you're much too small. Unless you're a child. That could be it. Are you?"

"No. I'm a gnome. I told you that, remember?"

"Oh right. A gnome. Little people. Love to tinker. Love to make inventions that never work. Most likely to die by flinging themselves out of some contraption or blowing themselves up. My father said gnomes are fun to talk to as long as you don't mind listening to them prattle on about their inventions. Have you ever invented something?"

Hector tried to say that he had, but his mouth wouldn't work right. He realized with alarm that the cactus juice he'd drunk was making his mind fuzzy and causing the ringing in his ears. The harder he tried to gather his thoughts the more they scattered into a thousand bits.

He wondered if Tumbleweed had remembered or even known the right dose to give to a gnome. Too much of a powerful elixir like that might very well kill him.

"So then this gnome my father met during the war invented these collapsible lances. They didn't work, of course." Tumbleweed's voice grew fainter and fainter as Hector's mind slipped away, overwhelmed by the medicine.

Chapter Eleven

Hector woke with a pounding headache. The rest of his body didn't feel so great either. Tumbleweed sat next to the dragon-sized stone bed, still talking. Hector kept his eyes closed and lay very still.

"So then, you see, the evil dragons stole most of the good dragon eggs. That's why most of the dragons you meet are old. My egg was laid after that. So I guess I'm pretty young as far as dragons go. But I'm big enough to look after myself. I have to now, anyway. Hey, are you awake?"

Hector cracked open his eyes. Tumbleweed must have heard a change in his breathing. "Yes. I am now, I guess."

"Great." Tumbleweed jumped up and went to the fire that still burned in the fireplace. "I have some food here for you." He lifted something long and thin out of the flames. "My father said gnomes eat meat. Not my preference, but easy enough to get out here."

"What is it?" Hector asked, though he wasn't sure he wanted to know.

"It's a cobra. You do like your meat cooked, don't you?"

Hector looked at the charred length of snake in Tumbleweed's claws. It was all he could do not to make a face, but his stomach rumbled with hunger. "Um . . . thanks," he said as Tumbleweed handed it over.

The hot snake burned his hands, and he dropped it on the rock and blew on it while he reached into his apron pocket for something to cut it with. His hands found only bandages.

"Where's my apron?" he cried in alarm.

"Apron?" Tumbleweed cocked his head to the side and eyed Hector dubiously.

"Yes, apron. The leather thing I was wearing with lots of pockets." The disappearance of his apron shook Hector more than he wanted to admit.

"Oh, something did fall off you when I clawed the centipedes from your chest. I suppose that must be it. It's probably back with the wagon. But why do you need that to eat?" Tumbleweed eyed Hector, waiting for him to explain.

"Nothing. Never mind." He didn't dare send Tumbleweed back to the wagon for fear of what the dragon might do to his supplies and equipment.

Hector tore the burned skin from the snake and nibbled the meat inside. It tasted something like chicken. Not too bad. He tucked in and filled his stomach, then realized that Tumbleweed was watching him eat, mesmerized.

Hector licked his fingers. "What about you?" He had no idea what brass dragons ate, but he figured a single snake couldn't satisfy its appetite.

Tumbleweed smiled and lifted a blue ceramic bowl from the hearth. "Dew drops," he said, licking his lips. "I gathered them off the cactus this morning."

"Dew drops? You can't be serious." Hector watched while Tumbleweed licked the sparkling water from the bowl. When Tumbleweed finished, he smacked his lips and belched, filling the chamber with the scent of burning metal.

Hector laughed, but that made his wounds hurt, and he winced.

"Still hurts, I see," Tumbleweed said. "I'm not surprised. Here." He offered Hector the wooden bowl, full again with the cactus juice.

Hector shook his head. "I'd rather be able to think straight. It doesn't hurt as bad now anyway. How long was I asleep?"

"Two days. Not long. Not nearly long enough to heal." Tumbleweed gave Hector a lopsided smile. "Don't you like it here? Isn't this place the most fabulous place you've ever been? You could settle down here, you know. Make it your home. I wouldn't mind."

Hector shuddered with the thought of living with the overeager dragon. "No. I'm afraid I can't. I have to get back to work. You see, I've invented this sender-receiver device. I tried to tell the humans about it, but they didn't understand. So now I have to set it up to prove to them it works."

"Oh good, humans. Tell me all about them," Tumbleweed said, lying down beside the rock and resting his chin inches away from Hector. His eyes glittered with anticipation.

"Never mind the humans," Hector said. "Take me back to my wagon." He didn't know how he could get his wagon away from where the centipedes were, or how he would pull it without a donkey. Perhaps he would have to get Tumbleweed to take him to Purespring to buy a new donkey. Of course, Kaal was closer, but Hector doubted they'd let him in the city again until after he proved his device would work.

A shock of fear went through Hector. He'd left the note for Shem to turn on the sender-receiver device in three weeks. A week and two days had already passed, and Hector didn't even have the line a quarter of the way to the mountains yet. Getting a new donkey would slow him down even further.

Tumbleweed growled deep in his throat, then stopped and smiled at Hector. "You can't leave yet," he said in a honey-sweet voice. "Your wounds haven't healed. There's no need to be in a big rush."

Hector slid to the edge of the stone bed and jumped down. The drop was farther than he'd anticipated. He hit the stone floor hard and crumpled over, gasping in pain and hoping he hadn't broken both of his legs.

Tumbleweed *tsk-tsked* him and lifted him back up onto the bed. "In a few days when you're feeling better, I'll show you around the lair. I know you're going to like it here."

"No, I'm not going to like it here," Hector shouted, wiggling out of his grasp. "I have to go. Please fly me to the nearest village."

Tumbleweed unfurled his wings and flapped them in agitation. Their movement sent sand and air spilling around the chamber. Hector covered his face to keep the abrasive material out of his eyes.

"I don't even know where the nearest village is!" Tumbleweed bellowed. "No way can I take you there." He stopped flapping and started pacing around and around the stone bed. "This is a wonderful lair. You will live here with me. We will talk about everything—the way the sun crosses the sky, how the desert beetle builds its tunnels. I'll tell you everything I know about the world, and you'll tell me everything you know."

Hector rubbed his throbbing legs and decided they weren't broken. He'd have to be more careful next time he tried to leave. He glared at Tumbleweed. For some reason the brass dragon seemed reluctant to let him go. Hector couldn't fathom why, but he knew he had to get out and finish his task with or without the dragon's help or permission.

CHAPTER TWELVE

Amber glared at the smelly stable yard where she had just been told—again—that her invention wouldn't work.

The mayor and his men had not found the thief who had stolen the Goodlunds' fabric two days before, though they searched the village and warned all the merchants to look for someone who might sell the bolt of blue silk.

The loss of the material had jeopardized the Goodlunds' business, and Amber couldn't bring herself to ask them for supplies to get home. She'd hoped to sell one of her inventions to finance her trip instead. Though she'd thought of several great ones, the villagers were reluctant to buy them.

A flash of red raced up the street toward Amber, and a second later Syndall skidded to a stop in front of her. "Amber, come quick. The thief has struck again. My mother's latest tapestry is missing, and it was supposed to go to a noble in Palanthas!"

"Impossible!" Amber cried. "No one could have gotten through my invincible-door-lock invention." A lump grew in her throat. Losing the tapestry would destroy the Goodlunds for sure.

"The thief didn't go through the door," Syndall said, motioning for Amber to hurry along with her as she headed for the mayor's house to report the theft. "He pried open a window. Don't ask me how in broad daylight with mother in the shop and all. One minute the tapestry was there on the shelf below the window, the next minute it was gone."

Amber ran behind Syndall. "How do you know the thief was a he?"

"Here." Syndall pulled out a white linen handkerchief and held it up for Amber to see. A large, roundish smudge marred the middle of the fabric.

"I don't understand." Amber tilted her head to get a different view of the smudge. "What does that have to do with the thief?"

"He must have sweated a lot while getting the window open, because he wiped his face on this fabric and accidentally dropped it on the shelf when he took the tapestry. And see, at the bottom of this smudge here are whisker marks. So unless some woman has sprouted whiskers, our thief is a man with a well-trimmed beard around two inches long."

Syndall marched up to the mayor's house and pounded on the door. While she related the whole story to the mayor, Amber's mind spun with all kinds of inventions she might use to catch the thief. She figured if he had stolen from the Goodlunds twice, he was sure to do it a third time.

"I have an idea," Amber told Syndall as soon as the mayor ran off, calling for the city militia. "Let's go to the shop and set some traps."

"Traps?" Syndall said. "How will that help?"

"Just trust me," Amber said.

"All right. Come on." Syndall took off down the street, making Amber run to keep up with her. They reached the shop, and Syndall stepped inside with Amber right behind. The acrid smell of material dyes almost overwhelmed her.

Syndall took a deep breath and let out a sigh. "I love that smell."

Amber wrinkled her nose and forced herself to ignore the dyes. She had work to do. Syndall hung about getting in the way while Amber bustled between the looms and spinning wheels.

"It really is a grand shop," Syndall said. She pointed to a bundle of fiber up against the right wall. "That's flax. Mother spins the flax into linen. That fluffy pile in the other bin is cotton. The next bin contains wool. Those cupboards there at the end hold silk thread. Very expensive.

You'll notice we have a lock on it—not that locks seem to stop this thief."

Amber nodded. They'd need something a lot more complicated.

Syndall continued talking while Amber got some rope and fashioned a pulley system. "Those shelves on the left wall over there are where she keeps the bolts of finished cloth, but we can't risk losing anything else. When I left, Mother and Father were moving the most valuable bolts up into their bedroom to guard them tonight."

"Good," Amber said.

Syndall ran a loving hand along the largest loom in the center of the shop. "Mother makes a wide variety of materials. She also knits and crochets and tats and all that. It's amazing."

"What about you?" Amber climbed up on the big loom to mount a pulley on the ceiling. "Do you plan to do the same when you get older, or will you be a fighter like your sister?" Syndall's older sister, Catriona, was the warrior who stopped the Bronze Giant and saved Kaal from its enemies.

Syndall wrinkled her nose and squinched her eyes closed in thought. After a moment her face relaxed and she smiled. "The Goodlunds have a proud history of Solamnic Knights and brilliant artisans. And if I had to choose between the two . . . I'd pick neither. Not right away at least. Though I've spent a lot of time learning my mother's trade, I'm just not ready to settle down yet. I don't want to be trapped here for the rest of my life with no chance to see all the wonders of the rest of the world."

Amber snorted.

Syndall waved a dismissive hand. "What about you? What will you do now that you've been banned from the Bronze Giant?"

"I'm going back home to work on my Life Quest."

"Where's Hector? If he got kicked out too, shouldn't he be headed back to Haggersmoore with you?"

Amber dropped her screwdriver. It clattered against the loom and clanged as it hit the floor. Muttering to herself, she climbed down to retrieve it. She didn't want to talk about Hector. Every time she even thought about him, her stomach twisted into a knot.

Before Syndall could ask any more questions, Amber marched over to the cupboard. "If everything valuable is put away, the thief is likely to assume it's locked in here. I think we'll focus the trap toward that and then put more around it, layer after layer. And something around your parents' room as well, just in case he thinks of that." Amber's mind spun with the details of her invention. Night would fall soon, and she didn't have much time left to build everything.

CHAPTER THIRTEEN

Hector rolled over as quietly as he could and looked at Tumbleweed's form atop the giant rock, checking for any sign that the dragon was still awake.

Tumbleweed had talked endlessly for hours, maybe even days. Hector couldn't be sure of the time he'd spent in the dragon's lair. It was always filled with the same red light from the fire in the great hearth—as if the place needed any more heat than what came from the desert sun outside.

The cave would have been almost cool, except for the fire. But Tumbleweed refused to let it die. He seemed to enjoy staring at the flames almost as much as talking.

That's what had given Hector an idea. He'd pretended to be cold up on the stone bed and asked Tumbleweed to let him sleep next to the fire. Tumbleweed had agreed, lifted Hector down, and laid him on the wide hearth before the fire.

Some hours later, after Tumbleweed's endless speech about desert flies, the dragon had stretched out on the rock and had asked Hector to tell him a little about his own home. Hector had launched into a long description of Haggersmoore and his father's home and inventions.

Gradually Tumbleweed had closed his eyes. Hector had kept talking and talking, and now, he was pretty sure Tumbleweed was asleep.

Hector rose. His aching body complained at the movement, but he wouldn't let that stop him. Time was slipping away, and he had to finish laying the line before Shem opened the letter.

He took a shaky step in the direction of the dark hole in the far wall he figured had to be the chamber's exit. His leg almost gave out on him. He swayed for a moment but stayed standing. Then he moved his other leg forward.

Step by slow step he crossed the chamber. The only sound was the crackle of the fire and Tumbleweed's light snoring.

As Hector neared the exit, he reached out to steady himself against the grainy sandstone wall. A little voice in the back of his head demanded to know how far he thought he could get out in the desert when he could barely walk across the one chamber unsupported.

He shoved the thought aside, but more insistent ones took its place: Where was the wagon? Which direction should he go when he got out? He had no idea where in the desert he was. And then if he did figure out which way to go to find the wagon, what about the centipedes, and how would he pull the wagon himself?

Shut up! he screamed at all the questions in his mind. One step at a time.

Still shaking and drenched in sweat, Hector eased into the dark tunnel that led from the sleep chamber. The ground was smooth and sandy beneath his feet. The afterimage of the fire still lingered in front of his eyes as he stared into the darkness.

One more step. He kept his hand on the wall and moved forward. One step. Then the next. And the next.

It was cooler out here in the tunnel than it had been in the chamber with the dragon and the fire. A faint air current stirred past him. The dragon's metallic smell lingered everywhere in the cave.

Hector made his way forward in the dark until the tunnel opened up into another chamber. Though he could not see, the room felt much bigger than the chamber he'd left behind. He paused, unsure if he should leave the wall and venture blindly across the vast expanse or follow the wall around. In the dark he had no way of knowing which direction to go to escape the dragon's lair.

He sucked in a worried breath.

"I know. Grand, isn't it?" Tumbleweed's voice sounded from right behind him. "It takes the breath away."

Hector jumped. So much for sneaking out. "I . . . um . . . I can't see anything," he stuttered.

"Right. Of course." Tumbleweed swept past him, lifting his wings so they went over Hector's head.

He heard the dragon walk forward a ways, then the footsteps changed to sound like they were going down stairs.

Tumbleweed sucked in a deep breath. Flame burst from his jaws, lighting the chamber. He sent the fire into a huge stone fireplace that made the one in the other room look child sized. Statues of two brass dragons wound around the massive fireplace. Their wings spread up along the wall above it, and their heads stared out across a gilded chamber. The room was shaped like a giant amphitheater with a glittering marble floor and steps leading up in a semicircle to where Hector stood.

Overhead, human-sized crystals protruded from the walls and ceiling, shimmering in a rainbow of colors cast by the fire. Hector gasped. He'd never seen anything quite so beautiful.

Tumbleweed sighed and ran his paw along the neck of one of the entwined brass statues. "My father paid a lot for these statues of him and my mother. Lovely, aren't they?" Tumbleweed frowned. "But they're not real. Not alive." He kicked the statue and then flapped away to land in the center of the massive chamber.

Hector stumbled over to the first step and sat down. "The hall is spectacular, Tumbleweed, but I need to go. I can't stay here."

Tumbleweed reared up, his eyes glowed like liquid metal. "No. You must stay. I won't be alone again. Never."

When he came down, his bared teeth glimmered in the firelight, and he advanced on Hector. "You will want for nothing here. I will provide you with whatever food you like. I'll bring you tools and equipment, and you can invent anything, everything. I won't criticize your work. I won't cast you out into the desert to die like whatever fools you lived with before."

"I wasn't exactly cast out," Hector argued. "All right, maybe I was, but Shem didn't send me out into the desert to die. I went there. I'm trying to make something, you see. And I need to finish."

"You can finish it here. I'll give you anything you want." Tumbleweed lowered his neck so his face was even with Hector's. "Anything. You name it."

"I want my freedom."

Tumbleweed reared up again, his wings undulating in fury. His roar filled the chamber, making Hector press his hands against his ears to muffle the sound.

"Right. Anything but that," Hector muttered.

Chapter Fourteen

Deep in the night the shop door creaked open. Amber crouched behind a thick spinning wheel near the back of the room. In the darkness, she could see a figure slip through the door, breathing heavily. He crawled across the room, his hands and knees making soft *pad pad* sounds on the wood floor.

Amber squinted to get a better look. Her mouth was dry in anticipation. The scent of the dye made her a little dizzy, but it wouldn't matter. Her traps would work all on their own.

She lost sight of the thief behind the looms, but she heard him sniffing. Sniffing? Strange, Amber thought. Maybe he has a cold. The thief padded to the back cupboard.

Perfect.

Staying low to the ground, he reached for the cupboard, still sniffing in his odd way.

Amber tensed. The thief moved the cupboard door,

92

and it pulled a string, which released a ball that went down a ramp, setting off her series of traps.

First, a heavy bolt of material fell on the thief.

He yelped and spun back for the door. That led him into a trip wire, which he somehow jumped over while still on his hands and knees. But on the far side of the wire he landed on an array of spools spread across the floor. They clattered and rattled as the thief tried to keep his balance.

He fell, thumping to the ground and letting out a weak whine as the air was knocked out of him. A weighted net dropped from the ceiling, blanketing the thief, who tried to get up but only succeeded in tangling himself in the net.

Unable to get away, the thief hunched, quivering, on hands and knees. Then he barked—deep angry yaps that filled the room with his misery.

"What?" Amber jumped to her feet. "Syndall, get the light."

A moment later the lamp flared to life. Right below it, in the center of the room, a scraggly, half-starved brown dog continued his angry barking.

Syndall groaned.

Amber shook her head. "Why would a dog wander into the shop and head right to the cupboard?"

"I don't know." Syndall reached out to get the net off

the dog and he snapped at her, almost biting off her fingers. "Stop it, you crazy dog!" she yelled.

Frowning, Amber eased over to the cupboard and swung it open. She scanned the shelf for anything out of place. There on the bottom, in the corner, was a bundle wrapped in dark brown fabric. When she picked it up, it squished in her hand. Blood seeped through the fabric and dripped on the floor.

"Eeew!" Amber dropped it. It plopped down and came unwrapped, revealing a juicy piece of beef.

The dog went crazy, biting at the net and scrambling to get to the meat. Amber kicked it over to him. Then she looked up at Syndall, and they both had the same thought.

"The house," Syndall cried, bolting to the door.

Amber raced after her. The thief would have to have put the meat in the cupboard while Syndall had gone to talk to the mayor after the tapestry went missing. He must have guessed Amber and Syndall would set a trap for him. He may have even watched in hiding while her parents carried the material inside the house.

Syndall slammed open the front door and ran to the hall that led upstairs to her parents' room. Amber followed, trying to keep up.

A desperate yowl filled the air, and a black streak shot out of the hall, almost bowling Amber over.

"A cat!" Ariana's voice carried across the house. "A cat sprung the traps in the hall."

Amber skidded to a stop and then reversed direction. That just left the trap outside the bedroom window.

Syndall raced past her.

They found Connal standing outside with a lantern. A bucket with its load of rocks still hung above the second-story window. The window ledge, set to break off if the thief climbed on it, sat intact. The spray of dirt that should have blinded him remained in its pouch beside the window.

But the window stood open. From inside the room, Ariana screamed. "It's gone! All of it gone."

Amber stared up at her in disbelief.

"He can't have gotten far with that load," Syndall murmured. "In fact, I don't see how he could have carried it himself at all. He must have a wagon."

Amber searched the road for signs of recent wagon tracks, but so many wagons traveled the road each day, and in the lantern's light she couldn't make out which might be the thief's.

"Couldn't have been a wagon," Connal said. "I was awake. I would have heard a horse or donkey outside my window. But there was no sound until the traps went off in the hall."

Amber clenched her fist inside her apron. She would have sworn on her life no thief would get past her traps. "I suppose he could have wrapped the horse's hooves in fabric and oiled the wagon so it wouldn't creak. The right kind of ladder could get him in and out of the window without setting off the traps." Blueprints for such a contraption spun through her mind.

"He'd need help though," Syndall said. "Someone to hand the material to, so he could get it out in the amount of time it took Mother to find the cat and Father to come out here with the lantern."

Unless he had some kind of contraption that would cinch the material all up in one bundle and leverage it out the window without ever going in. Amber doubted the thief could make something that complicated.

"Look at this." Syndall knelt and pointed to a ragged print in the sand. "That could be the horse's print if its hooves were wrapped in fabric. It's different enough with the material that we could follow it."

"Good," Connal said. "I'll go wake the mayor and get some help. You girls follow that path and find the thief. As soon as you locate him, one of you come get me and the others. Don't confront him yourselves. We'll surround him and then capture him."

"I guess I'll stay here and clean up the mess," Ariana said, frowning.

"Great. Let's go, Amber." Syndall took the lantern and started off.

Amber went after her, calling back to Ariana, "Be careful with the dog in the shop. It bites."

They hurried down the row of houses to where the road turned to go into the heart of town. Just past the turn, Syndall stopped and picked something up from the middle of the road. She held out a torn piece of burlap.

"He took the padding off the horse's hooves. Now his tracks will look like all the others."

Amber groaned. The streets lay empty as far as she could see. No sound interrupted the night's silence except her rough breathing. The thief had escaped again.

Hector strolled down the long hall filled with what Tumbleweed called his parents' treasure. In truth, here and there Hector caught sight of some things other dragons might consider treasure. A golden bowl, a diamond necklace, a strange vase with steel coins affixed to the outside in an odd pattern. At least the steel had value.

The other objects in the hall baffled Hector. The dragons seemed to have collected a wide variety of fabrics. There was a huge tapestry on the wall depicting the forests of the Vingaard Mountains. Not far from the tapestry he saw a twisted piece of wood and a collection of leaves in a display box.

"What do you think?" Tumbleweed rumbled, pleased with the hall.

Hector fumbled for an answer. What could he say? This was like no treasure hoard he'd ever imagined. He looked away from the dubious treasure to the tunnel at the far end of the hall and wondered if that might be a way out.

Tumbleweed wrapped a claw around Hector's chest. "Don't think of trying to run away again. I'm much bigger than you, and much faster."

Hector twisted out of his grasp and turned to glare at him. "I'll tell you what I think. My father has more treasure in the chest he keeps locked up under his bed than this whole batch all together. You're just a selfish little dragon. I know why the blue dragon didn't kill you too. You weren't worth the bother. He figured you wouldn't survive long on your own anyway."

Hector stomped back to the Grand Conversation Hall and slumped down on the steps. Tumbleweed left him alone for a while before sliding in, down the steps, and turning around so his head came even with where Hector sat.

"You don't like me, do you?" Tumbleweed said in a doleful voice.

"Of course I don't like you," Hector answered. "You're keeping me prisoner."

"No, no. Not a prisoner. A guest." Tumbleweed's wings fluttered, creating a cool breeze in the chamber.

"A prisoner." Hector folded his arms across his chest and turned his back to the dragon.

"Aw, come on," Tumbleweed said. "We've had such great conversations. It's good to have someone to talk to, isn't it? You must feel the same way."

Hector thought about how lonely he'd been in Kaal until Amber showed up. It had been nice to have someone in the lab to work with and to talk to. He couldn't argue with Tumbleweed on that point, but the dragon was so full of himself, always talking, always interrupting even when he'd asked Hector to tell him something, never listening to what Hector said.

Hector turned back to face Tumbleweed. It felt weird looking straight into the dragon's glowing eyes. "Our conversations might be nice to you, but not to me. You never listen to what I'm saying. You don't try to understand what's really important to me. You're just a spoiled brat."

Tumbleweed backed away from him and shook his massive, plated head. "Why should I care about your silly little inventions? You stupid gnome. Run off back into the desert and get yourself killed. I'll find someone else to be my friend." Tumbleweed folded his wings tight against his sides and stormed out of the hall, leaving Hector alone.

Hector's face grew hot and he sprang to his feet to shout another insult at the dragon, then it sank in what Tumbleweed had said. Hector was free. He could go.

He ran down the steps to the fire and lit a long piece of wood for a torch. Then he raced back up, passed through the hall with the dragons' hoard, and hurried into the tunnels beyond.

CHAPTER FIFTEEN

The flames from the burning wood lit the tunnel with an eerie light, casting shadows on the walls as Hector searched for a way out. The thick sand on the floor made walking difficult, but he had grown used to sand in his shoes from his time setting up the wire in the desert.

He came to an intersection where three other tunnels branched out. Which way to go? He glanced back the way he'd come, fearing Tumbleweed might change his mind and come after him. The tunnel remained empty, though Tumbleweed's metallic smell lingered everywhere in the lair.

Hector licked his lips and stepped into the tunnel to the right. It occurred to him he should have at least gotten some water from the pond in the resting chamber before setting out into the desert. But he had nothing practical to carry it in. No sense going back.

He came to another split and went right again, hoping he was going in the correct direction. Ahead he saw a faint glow of golden light. He rushed forward and found a wall of sand. The light came from the other side just beyond.

This had to be the exit. Hector figured Tumbleweed used the thin layer of sand over the hole to hide it from enemies such as the blue dragon that had killed his parents.

Poor baby dragon. All alone.

Hector gritted his teeth. He couldn't stay and play nursemaid to a dragon. He had to finish laying the line to the dwarf kingdom before it was too late.

He took a deep breath and stepped forward, but his own voice in his head stopped him: *You never listen to what I'm saying. You don't try to understand what's really important to me.* That's what he'd told Tumbleweed, and it was true, but he'd heard those words before. Amber had said them during their last argument before they split up to go their separate ways.

Hector sucked in a sharp breath. Amber. Could it be true that he'd treated Amber the same way Tumbleweed treated him? Always talking. Never listening.

He'd done the same thing with the dragon. Even while listening to Tumbleweed talk, he'd never paid attention. He'd spent most of the time thinking how he could get the dragon to listen to him instead. Now in anger he'd alienated Tumbleweed into letting him go, but what good was his new freedom?

Outside the lair lay the vast desert. He had no idea which way to go to find his wagon, no way to pull it if he did find it, no way to even get past the centipedes.

Grumbling, he kicked at the sand on the tunnel floor. It would be crazy to go out into the desert alone with no supplies. He needed the dragon, but couldn't think how he could convince Tumbleweed to help him.

A sharp pain on his hand reminded him he carried a burning stick. The flames had worked their way down to his fingers.

"Ouch!" he cried and dropped the makeshift torch. The fire went out, leaving only the dim light that came through the sand covering the exit.

He turned away from it and stared back into the tunnel. He should find Tumbleweed and apologize. The thought scared him. A happy, silly dragon was imposing enough. An angry dragon would be terrifying.

From down the tunnel, he heard a soft whisper of sand, then Tumbleweed's voice. "Hector?" The dragon's plaintive tone kept Hector from dashing out the exit in fear. He stood frozen for a moment, unable to answer, struggling to find something to say.

Tumbleweed stepped into the dim light and hunched down, lowering his head to talk to Hector. His long pointed tongue flicked in and out several times and then he said, "I'm sorry. You're right. I have been selfish."

Hector's jaw dropped. "I . . . um . . . I think I have been too. Sorry," he blurted out.

The dragon's lips curled up into a smile, showing his sharp white teeth. "Do you think we can be friends? I promise I won't keep you here if you don't want to stay."

Hector shuffled his feet and rubbed his bald head. "Well actually, I could use a friend just now. I don't think I can set up my invention all by myself."

Tumbleweed reached out his claw and encircled Hector, edging him closer. "Why don't you tell me all about it?"

The dragon's scales were cool and comfortable against Hector's back. "You really want to know?"

Tumbleweed blinked and let out a puff of warm air. "What are you doing out in the desert that is so important?"

With his heart beating so loud it almost drowned out his voice, Hector explained to Tumbleweed about his device, what it could do, and why it was important.

Tumbleweed listened, nodding intently with his tongue lolling out one side of his mouth.

"But you see my problem now," Hector said. "With the donkey gone, I can't pull the wagon. And the centipedes . . ." He shuddered. His wounds ached just thinking about the horrible creatures.

"I have an idea," Tumbleweed said. "What if I help you lay the line across the desert?"

"Oh would you?" Hector clapped his hands in delight.

"I would, on one condition," Tumbleweed said, his voice serious and low.

Hector caught his breath. "What condition?"

A half smile played on Tumbleweed's face, and his eyes twinkled. "First you string the wire to my lair and set up one of your talking machines here. It's pretty much on your path to the dwarf kingdom anyway. That way you and I can always stay in contact."

Hector's heart sank. "I don't have an extra sender-receiver device made right now and no supplies to make one. I just have the one to set up for Goldmane."

Tumbleweed licked his sharp teeth. "But you could make another one for me after you've proved yourself to the humans and dwarves, right?"

"Well sure, I could make another one. Just not right now." Hector felt uncomfortably close to the dragon's mouth. Tumbleweed could swallow him in a single bite.

"Good." Tumbleweed stood and stretched. "I'll help you run the line to my lair and then over to the mountains. I think you can get it done a lot faster than before with my help, and I'll protect you from anything that tries to get in the way."

He flicked his tongue out boldly, but then a worried look crossed his face. "Almost anything."

Hector didn't need to ask what "almost anything" meant. He could guess from the look of fear in Tumbleweed's eyes. With all his dragon strength and speed, he would still be no match for the blue dragon that had killed his parents.

Hector patted his leg. "With any luck, we won't have to worry about that."

"Right. We could get lucky. Let's go." Tumbleweed grabbed Hector up in his claw and ducked through the wall of sand.

Golden grains rushed over Hector, getting inside his clothes and covering his face. It lasted only for a moment though, then he and Tumbleweed burst out of the lair into the desert light. The morning sun glowed on the eastern horizon, painting the rock towers over Tumbleweed's lair red, orange, and pink.

Tumbleweed launched into the air, and Hector gasped. The ground sped by below him in a wash of color. Tumbleweed roared with delight as they flew across the desert.

CHAPTER SIXTEEN

Amber walked with Syndall to the stable yard. On the way, they passed a band of town militia. Determination glinted in the villagers' eyes. Since the break-in last night, the mayor had closed the roads out of town. All morning his men had searched every house in the village and now were searching each wagon and every visitor to Purespring.

Syndall's parents were already with the mayor in the stable yard, interviewing a group of Solamnic Knights who had journeyed to Purespring to see the temple and bathe in the healing waters from the spring.

Amber followed Syndall up to the group and stopped. She might have felt tired from staying up all night searching for the thief, but her mind kept working on the problem, replaying everything that had happened in the house and the shop, trying to figure out how the thief could have managed to pull off the heist.

"Why have you detained us?" the oldest knight asked, bringing Amber's thoughts back to the moment. The knight's hair was gray, and from the look of the scar on his face and the way he limped on his right leg, he needed a well-deserved vacation to Purespring. His gray eyes looked tired, as if they'd seen too much fighting.

He and the other five knights with him were all clean shaven. They'd come into town just the day before. Amber doubted any of them could be involved with the thief, but the mayor and his helpers were checking everyone.

"A thief has stolen some valuable articles, Sir Guyon," the mayor said. No one had dared confront the knights without the mayor present, since Guyon was a high-ranking Knight of the Crown. Now the mayor spoke to him with great courtesy and respect. "I'm afraid we are going to have to search your trunks and saddlebags."

"Are you accusing us of stealing?" A younger knight jerked his sword out of its sheath and stepped toward the mayor. "How dare you question our honor?"

"No. No." The mayor lifted his hands. "Of course we don't think you stole the fabric, but the thief might have hidden the stolen property in your things, intending to get it later. We need to search everywhere. My men even looked through my home. Please, let them check your bags."

Sir Guyon lifted his hand. "Put your sword away, Frederick. They have not insulted our honor. They merely seek to catch a thief. Of course you may go through our things, Mayor. Then we will help you search everyone else. Such villainy must be punished."

Still scowling, the younger knight sheathed his sword. But the sharp look on Sir Guyon's face made Amber shiver. She'd hate to be in the thief's shoes when the knights caught up with him.

While Sir Guyon opened each of their trunks and bags for the mayor, another group of villagers went through the tedious process of searching the merchant wagons of the train from Kaal.

Foss leaned against his wagon, watching as the men pulled several small jars of herbs from the back. "You think a whole bolt of material would fit in that little jar?" he joked.

Amber laughed. She liked Foss and doubted he would have anything to do with a thief.

Shoved aside in a far corner of the stable yard, lost in the hubbub and mess from the search, a lone girl stood next to a rickety little wagon. Amber wandered in that direction. On the back of the wagon was a boxy little house, so shabby it might fall apart at any moment. The wagon sagged on its axles, its bottom low to the ground.

A group of townsmen opened the house's cracked wooden door and searched inside. It took them about ten seconds. Through the open door, Amber could see there was barely room inside for a miniature woodstove, a small chest, and a pile of straw for sleeping on, with only a couple of burlap bags for blankets and a worn-out bearskin. The chest held nothing more than a change of clothes and a chipped plate and cup.

The girl stood next to the wagon, her brown hair dirty and tangled. But it was her face that drew Amber's attention. It was horribly scarred all along one side as if burned in some intense fire. After a moment, Amber realized the fire had touched more than her face—the girl's right arm and hand were equally disfigured.

Amber felt bad for her. She must have come to town to seek the healing waters at the temple. Amber hoped she had enough steel to get in, or that the temple priestess, the Mother of Waters, would allow her entrance anyway.

"No luck," Syndall said, coming up to Amber. "They've searched everywhere. Every house, every wagon, everything. The material has just vanished."

"Can I have your attention, please?" The mayor's voice rose above the crowd.

More than one frustrated merchant glared at him. The hot sun filled the stable yard, along with enough dust from everyone milling around to make Amber sneeze.

After the mayor had everyone's attention, he continued speaking. "I apologize for any stress and inconvenience this search may have caused. Purespring values all merchants and visitors, especially those who have come to seek the healing waters of the spring. In restitution for your time and keeping those of you here who were planning to leave this morning, I would like to invite you all over to the Sandway Inn for a free meal. I ask, though, that if any of you see or hear news of the Goodlunds' fabrics, you send word to me so the thief can be brought to justice."

Syndall chuckled. "The mayor has always been fond of speeches."

"I like the sound of free food," Amber said, anxious to get out of the dusty stable yard. Together she and Syndall made their way to the inn.

The Sandway Inn was nothing more than a mud-brick hovel with its thatched roof and slightly off-square windows. Inside it was as hot and crowded as any place was sure to be when free food was offered.

Amber and Syndall squeezed in at a square table near the back where Sir Frederick and Sir Guyon sat talking with Foss and another merchant. The ragged girl Amber had seen in the stable yard sat hunched on the floor behind them, her back to the corner and her knees up to her chest.

The innkeeper's wife carried a tray of steaming rolls and tender cooked beef to the table. "How are you holding up?" she asked Syndall, giving the choicest cut of meat to her and patting her shoulder.

"I'm all right," Syndall said, but Amber knew that the loss of the fabric was a hard blow to the Goodlunds. Without the income from selling it, they wouldn't be able to buy enough supplies to keep the shop open. Amber wished there was more she could do for Syndall, but Syndall just motioned to the food.

"Eat," she told Amber.

With nimble fingers, Amber filled her plate before the bigger knights and merchants could take all the food. As she stuffed a roll in her mouth, she noticed out of the corner of her eye that the girl in the corner still had no food.

Amber grabbed a plate containing the scraps of what was left, slid down from her chair, and went over to the girl. "Here," she said, holding out the plate. "You won't get anything sitting down there."

The girl shook her head. "I don't deserve any." She lowered her dirty face against her knees as if ashamed to have anyone see her scars.

Amber snorted. "Well, you get some whether you think you deserve it or not." She grabbed the girl's hand and wrapped her fingers around the plate. "Go on. Eat it. It's not much anyway."

"Thank you," the girl murmured, looking even more miserable than before.

Amber gave her an encouraging smile and returned

to the table where Foss was telling an animated story to the knights.

"Right. So this gnome wheels this device into the hall and says he's found a way to create and control lightning. We all laughed. I mean really, he's a gnome. How often do any of their inventions work?"

"More often than you might think," Sir Guyon whispered so low only Amber, who sat right next to him, could hear. He gave Amber a wink without taking his attention off the merchant and his story.

Amber cringed. She knew where the story was going and didn't want to hear the end of it.

"So what happened?" Syndall asked, eager for Foss to continue.

Amber stuffed beef into a roll and took a big bite, letting the rich flavor soothe her nerves. Everyone was listening now. There was no way she could stop the merchant from telling his tale.

"So the gnome cranks this lever, and the machine does something that fills the room with the smell that you get in a thunderstorm just before lightning strikes. Except we don't see any sign of lightning. No bolts of power, no sound of thunder. The machine just sits there."

Everyone at the table laughed, except Amber.

Amber's face grew hot. She put down her sandwich and glared at Foss. "But Hector's lightning machine does work," she shouted over the top of their laughter.

Sir Guyon fell silent and looked down at her. The others continued to snicker.

"It's true," Amber insisted. "You tell them," she ordered Foss.

Foss lifted his hand and stopped laughing. The others gave Amber a patronizing look and waited for him to finish the story.

"It's true," Foss said. "Amber is right. The invention did work. When the leader of Kaal touched it, the lightning blasted him across the room and almost killed him."

The table fell silent. Everyone stared at Foss. "It's true," he said weakly, as if unsure now how to make them believe him.

Sir Guyon got to his feet. "I'm sure it is." He put a firm hand on Amber's shoulder. "Hector built it, you say?"

"Well, yes. Do you know him?" Amber asked. Most humans pretended gnomes didn't exist. She was surprised a Solamnic Knight knew Hector's name.

The knight gave Amber a grim smile. "Oh yes. I know him. He and his father have a contract with us to build new weapons. But Hector's supposed to be dead. And his father hasn't invented anything for us since he heard about his son's death—nothing, though he keeps saying he's working on it and keeps taking our steel. So I'm very glad to hear Hector is alive and has invented something useful."

He dropped his hand from Amber's shoulder to rest on his sword hilt. "Imagine what we could do if we armed all of our units with such a lightning machine." He laughed, a grim and brittle sound.

Amber jumped up on her chair. "No. It's not a weapon."

But the knight just waved for her to be quiet. "Is Hector still in Kaal?" he asked Foss.

Foss shook his head. "They kicked him out. He was supposed to come to Purespring with us and his little friend here, but he went off into the desert instead."

Sir Guyon frowned. "He might be hard to find in the desert. Any idea where he was heading? He owes us an invention or two, and this sounds like just the thing to settle the debt."

"No. No. No!" Amber cried. "It's not a weapon. It's his Life Quest. You can't take it."

Foss cleared his throat. "I doubt you'll have any trouble finding him at all. Since I joined the train late, I watched him go out into the desert from the back of the city wall. He's stringing some sort of wire across the wasteland. If you want to find Hector, all you have to do is start at Kaal and follow the wire."

Amber choked. Foss had been so nice to her, but just like many humans she'd met, he didn't understand how important Hector's Life Quest was.

"Thank you," Sir Guyon said, bowing to Foss. Then he pivoted away from the table and strode out of the room with Sir Frederick on his heels.

Chapter Seventeen

Kyani curled his wings and flipped over and over in a series of barrel rolls. Though clutched safely in the dragon's front paw, Hector screamed. "Stop! You're making me sick."

Kyani laughed and snapped back upright. Clouds of golden sand flared up below him as he flew. Overhead the hot blue sky radiated across his back, making him happy. Or perhaps it was the new friend he carried with him.

He flew only a yard or two above the sand dunes. He'd tried to go higher, but between Hector's weight and his immature wings, he couldn't rise much farther off the ground. A wiggly, scared feeling in his gut warned him that staying low was better anyway. If he flew too high, he could be seen for miles and miles, a bright glitter of brass in the sky.

Rumbling deep in his chest, he dropped lower, letting his tail slide along the tips of the dunes like a snake through the sand. He loved the way the hot granules felt against his scales and the sound of the hiss as he lifted from one dune to the next.

"Are you getting tired?" Hector asked. "Do you need to rest or drink some water?"

"No. I'm fine," Kyani said.

A little black beetle scuttled down the dune in front of him. Kyani called a cheerful hello as he flew over. "Hello, bug. Hello, sand. Hello, sky. Hello, sun." He pulled himself up so he could feel the sun on his chest and did a backward somersault in the air.

"Tumbleweed!" Hector cried. "Put me down."

Kyani laughed and settled onto the warm sand, releasing Hector.

His little gnome friend took a step, wavered, and tumbled forward.

Hector pushed himself up with his hands and emptied his stomach on the sand. Groaning, he rolled away from the mess and stared up at Kyani. "I bet there are a lot of folks who would love a ride like that," he said, his voice raspy. "I think I'll invent one as long as I don't have to ride on it."

"Feeling better?" Kyani asked. A tiny niggle of guilt suggested he should have flown a bit more smoothly for his friend.

"I'll be fine as soon as the world stops spinning." Hector took a deep breath and blinked his eyes. "How far are we from the wagon?"

Kyani dug his claws into the sand and hung his head. "Only about halfway there. If I were bigger, I could go a lot faster."

"But at this rate, we should get there just before dark. That's perfect. We'll be able to take care of the centipedes while we can still see them, then get to work on the line when things cool down." Hector paused. "Any idea what we're going to do about the centipedes?"

Kyani lifted his head and pranced in a circle. "Last time, I used my sleep breath on them. I love that. The little critters fell right to sleep, and I didn't even have to hurt them. Of course you fell asleep too, so I couldn't talk to you all the way back to the lair."

"I think I'm glad I was asleep at that point." Hector rubbed the bandages on his arms and chest. Kyani could tell the centipede bites still hurt Hector, but the gnome had refused any more cactus juice.

Hector got to his feet, swaying a little. He put his hands on his head and stood very still for a few moments, then he shook himself and nodded to Kyani. "All right, Tumbleweed, let's go. But this time, can you just fly straight and smooth?"

"I'll try." Kyani curled his claw around Hector. "Maybe someday you'll like my aerobatics."

"I doubt it," Hector said as Kyani launched back into the air.

Amber marched to the edge of Purespring with Syndall, who was still stuffing things into a small pack.

"Do you have to go so soon?" Syndall asked. "It's not your fault the thief got away with the material. You tried. We all tried. Why don't you stay awhile?" She stopped and held the pack out to Amber. Ariana had filled it with food and water, a cloak, and an extra change of clothes.

"Thank you," Amber said, taking the pack. "I'm sorry I can't stay, and I'm sorry about the stolen fabric. But Hector's in trouble, and I need to warn him."

"Oh, I don't think those knights will be any problem. It's just one little invention. They won't go after it, will they?" Syndall's forehead wrinkled.

"I'm afraid they will," Amber said, slipping the pack onto her back. It was heavy, but she knew she wouldn't survive in the desert without those supplies. She didn't even have anything to pay the Goodlunds for it, but she vowed someday she'd reimburse them.

"Hector's machine is more than a little invention," she explained. "If it works the way he wants it to, it could change the world for good. If the knights get ahold of it and use it as a weapon, it will ruin everything. I didn't understand why he wouldn't take it back to Haggersmoore.

But then I didn't know about his father's contract with the knights. He should have told me they'd want to take his invention and use it to kill."

Amber plunged her hands into her apron pocket and fingered her favorite wrench. The motion made her bracelet jingle, and she felt even worse about leaving Hector. Ahead of her lay the road into the desert. A mile or so out, she could see the diminishing figures of the mounted knights as they trotted along the road to Kaal. She'd never be able to catch them. Their horses were too fast, and she had to go on foot. But she didn't need to catch them to warn Hector. She just had to get to Kaal in time.

"Good-bye, Syndall," she said, hugging her friend around the waist. "Thanks for the pack. I owe you one."

"Just be careful, all right?" Syndall said, returning the hug. "I don't want anything bad to happen to you."

"Don't worry." Amber walked away, waving good-bye one more time over her shoulder. She hurried down the road, ignoring the hot sun on her back and the cloud of dust that puffed up around her feet. Far ahead, the knights disappeared over the horizon. Hector's bracelet jingled on her wrist with each step. Her heart beat fast, urging her on.

She pictured all the horrible things the knights could do with Hector's invention. They were right. It could be a dangerous weapon, providing the ability to kill with lightning, but without the physical limitations the wizards faced from their magic spells. Poor Hector. He'd planned his device to stop wars, not fight them.

"Hey there." A soft voice beside Amber made her jump. She'd been staring ahead and hadn't noticed anyone coming behind. Now she saw that the ragged girl she'd seen in Purespring had joined her on the road, wagon and all.

A gray horse pulled the wagon. Muscles bulged along its legs and chest. It held its head high and walked so lightly that it seemed to float above the sand.

"Oh," Amber said. "You snuck up on me." She wondered how such a rickety old wagon could move without any sound. The girl must have taken great pains to make sure the axle stayed greased and free from sand. The tiny house on the back wobbled a bit with each prancing step the horse took.

"Sorry," the girl said. She sat on a narrow bench at the front of the wagon, holding the reins loose in her hands. She looked out across the desolate land of rocks and sage and cacti. "What are you doing out here? I mean, it's none of my business, but it's a big desert and a long way to walk on foot." She gave Amber a worried look.

Out in the sun away from the city and people, the girl seemed more relaxed and confident. Amber thought that perhaps she worried what people would think of her scarred face. Not that it bothered Amber. Hector had lost all his hair in a fire, after all, and she still liked him. She shuddered at the thought of Hector being burned as bad as the girl must have been.

"I guess you don't have to tell me if you don't want to." The girl pulled back on the reins, slowing the horse so it stayed beside Amber a moment longer.

Amber started, realizing she hadn't answered the girl's question. "Oh sorry. I was just thinking. I—"

"It's my face, isn't it?" the girl said, bitterly. "It bothers everyone. No one wants to look at me, let alone talk to me. But I thought . . . well, back there you actually . . ." She looked down at her hands. "Oh, never mind." She twitched the reins, and the horse started into a trot. The wagon pulled ahead of Amber.

"No wait!" Amber called. "It's not like that. I was just thinking of someone. My friend. My best friend. He was burned in a fire."

The wagon slowed and the girl turned back to Amber. "You don't mind my face?"

"No. Of course not." Amber gave her a reassuring smile.

The wagon stopped. The girl dropped the reins and jumped to the ground in front of Amber. The horse stood still though the girl had done nothing to keep it from running off with the wagon.

"My name is Dani. What's yours?" She held out her burned, shriveled hand to the gnome.

"Amber." Amber took her hand, feeling the uneven scars press against her palm. "And I have to get to Kaal as soon as possible to help my friend. I think he's in trouble."

"Funny. That's where I'm going too. Why don't you hop up and come along with me? Felicity won't mind a little extra weight on the wagon."

"Felicity," Amber said, stepping up to the big animal. "Funny name for a horse. Especially a male. Seems like a good horse though. Very strong."

"Oh yes, and fast," Dani said. "My father created this breed of horses for work in the desert. Nothing beats them in this type of terrain. And Felicity was my father's best stud when he was younger." Dani patted Felicity's back. Then she picked Amber up and swung her onto the wagon bench. "There you go."

"Thanks," Amber said. Dani didn't look it, but she was as strong as her horse. She climbed up beside Amber, took the reins, and nodded to Felicity. The horse nodded back and broke into a trot without Dani even moving the reins.

"That's amazing," Amber said. "Your father must be an incredible breeder and trainer."

Dani frowned, looked away from Amber, and rubbed her eyes. "Stupid sand. Always getting in my face," she muttered.

Amber didn't say anything, but she was pretty sure it wasn't the sand that made Dani's eyes water. "What happened to your father?" Amber whispered.

Dani had to turn away again for a moment. Then she cleared her throat and clenched the reins tight in her hands. "My family was killed by a dragonlord, the same one who demolished so many other villages around here. A lot of people got hauled off as slaves. But my father tried to fight. The dragon burned our house, killed my family, and ate the horses. Old Felicity and I survived just out of pure luck. We'd gone for a ride in the desert that morning. When we came back, the house was on fire. I tried to save my family, but—" Dani shook her head and bit her lip.

Amber reached over and patted her burned hand. "I'm sorry."

They rode in silence for a while. Finally Dani sniffed, rubbed her eyes one last time, and smiled. "But I'm not giving up. I survived. I'm going to make a good life for myself. Even better than my father had. I'll get enough steel to have a big mansion and fill it with all sorts of beautiful things. This"—she waved at the little box house behind her—"is just the beginning. I'll have all the food I want and . . . well, everything."

"Sounds wonderful." Amber decided not to ask how she intended to become so rich with a rickety old cart and a horse past his prime. Better to let Dani have her little daydream if it made her happy.

CHAPTER EIGHTEEN

Hector squinted at the horizon as the sunlight dimmed. At the edge of the vast nothingness, he could make out scattered boulders and a tall cactus. Below them hunched the blocky silhouette of his wagon.

"There it is," he cried.

Tumbleweed gripped him tighter and redoubled his speed, his wings whipping the dunes below them. Hector wrapped his arms around Tumbleweed's scaly claws. His stomach twisted. He didn't mind flying as long as it was smooth and straight with no crazy rolls. He'd made his own flying machine, after all, though the windstorm had destroyed it. But the thought of facing the centipedes again made him feel nauseous.

"Don't worry," Tumbleweed rumbled. "I'll take care of those nasty creatures."

With a whoosh of air, Tumbleweed landed on the rocky ground beside the cart. Poor Thistle lay dead. Only his bones remained. Hector swallowed a lump in his throat. Thistle had been a good and loyal donkey.

"Hold your breath," Tumbleweed said. "I'm going to gas the centipedes. Don't want you to fall asleep too." Hector put his hand over his mouth and nose while Tumbleweed blew out a billowing cloud of smoke. It surrounded the wagon, working its way around the rocks and into tunnels where the centipedes might be hiding.

Hector's lung screamed for air, but he dared not breathe at the moment. He tapped on Tumbleweed's claw and motioned for him to take to the air. Tumbleweed jumped up with Hector and, flapping his wings, hovered over the cloud.

Hector gasped. "Hope that works."

After a moment the smoke dissipated and Tumbleweed landed again. He opened his claw and set Hector on the ground. Hector's legs felt like jelly, and he wobbled for a moment with the feeling that he was still flying.

"You all right?" Tumbleweed asked.

"Yes. Sure." As soon as his legs decided to cooperate, he lifted his fallen apron from the ground. It felt heavy and uneven in his hand. He reached in to resituate his tools, and a cluster of feathery legs covered his hand.

He screamed and dropped the apron. "A centipede. Get it out. Get it out."

Tumbleweed laughed, picked up the apron, and shook it upside down. Hector's tools clattered to the ground—along with a peacefully sleeping centipede.

"Here." Tumbleweed handed him the apron.

Keeping his eye on the centipede, Hector gathered his tools and slipped them back into his pockets, then tied on the apron.

"Maybe I better check the wagon for centipedes as well," Tumbleweed said.

"No, wait. Be careful. You might break something," Hector cried.

Tumbleweed paused with his claw over the covered sender-receiver device. "I can be careful. I'm not some big clumsy monster, you know. I'm a dragon." Delicately he pulled back the cover and sniffed around in the wagon bed. He found four centipedes while Hector fetched the ladder he'd dropped on the night of the attack.

Hector eased the ladder into the back of the wagon beside the pile of poles. Then, glancing nervously at the ground, he checked his copper wire from the thick coil in the wagon up to the top of the last cactus where he'd attached it. He gazed at the line stretching back in gentle arcs from cactus to cactus to Kaal. It looked all right.

"What now?" Tumbleweed asked.

Hector pulled a compass from his pocket and held it out. The needle spun back and forth for a moment, then came to rest. Hector took his bearing and pointed across the sand dunes in the direction he needed to put his next post. "We go that way. You'll have to pull the wagon, I'm afraid."

Tumbleweed snorted and reached out to grab both sides and lift it.

"No!" Hector shouted in alarm. "Don't pick it up. You'll dump everything and tear out the line."

Tumbleweed rippled his wings in agitation. "If you don't want me to pick it up, how am I supposed to move it?"

Hector grimaced and went over to Thistle's bones. Fortunately the harness was still intact. He eased it off Thistle and held it out. "You can pull the wagon."

Tumbleweed shook his head and reared up so the last rays of the setting sun glimmered off his chest. "Pull the wagon like a common horse? No way. Besides, that harness won't fit me."

Hector rubbed his head, wondering how to convince Tumbleweed to draw the wagon. Out of the corner of his eye, he saw a shadow move. He jumped. "Tumbleweed, I think the centipedes are waking up. We've got to get out of here. Please, just hold the harness and pull the wagon. That's not like a horse. You'll be majestic and beautiful and helpful and kind."

Tumbleweed settled back onto his legs and growled deep in his chest, his molten eyes fixed on Hector.

A scuttling sound came from the rocks behind Hector, and he whipped around, trying to see the centipede in the near darkness. "Tumbleweed, please," he said, his voice strained. "I'll let you talk the whole time. We'll have a grand conversation."

Tumbleweed's eyes narrowed for a moment, then he snorted, took the harness in his front claw, and motioned for Hector to climb on the wagon. Hector scrambled onto the seat and pointed in the direction they needed to go.

Walking on three legs and pulling with the forth, Tumbleweed set out across the sand, jabbering about an incoherent array of topics. The wagon jerked and stopped, jerked and stopped with each stride. Tumbleweed's body was not made for pulling things, and he leaped forward in quick, hopping motions.

At first, Hector found the movement uncomfortable, but he soon got used to it. He had Tumbleweed stop at the top of a dune the right distance from the last cactus.

He hopped off the wagon, went around back, and got his shovel. Tumbleweed watched as Hector plunged it into the ground, lifted it back up, and tossed the sand aside. He scooped out a second and third load, but each time he scooped, the sand around the edges slid down, filling the hole.

Grunting in annoyance, he set aside the shovel and dug with his hands as fast as he could. Still the sand filled in everything he lifted out.

Tumbleweed paced around him. "What are you trying to do?" he asked.

"I have to dig this hole so I can put one of those poles

in and string up that wire there," Hector said, his frustration ringing in his voice.

Tumbleweed cocked his head to one side. "You want the pole stuck in the ground?"

"Yes. I just said that."

Tumbleweed's claw wrapped around Hector and lifted him away from the hole he was trying to dig.

"Hey!" Hector shouted.

Still holding Hector in one paw, Tumbleweed reached into the back of the wagon with the other and lifted out a pole. He leaped into the air and came back down, plunging the pole deep into the sand. When he let go, it stood straight and unmoving.

Hector blinked in surprise and asked Tumbleweed to put him down. The dragon complied. Hector walked over to the pole and pushed it. It seemed secure. He put his shoulder against it and tried to knock it over. It refused to budge.

"You did it!" he whooped with delight.

Tumbleweed smiled and picked up Hector. Then he lifted the copper wire where it trailed from the back of the wagon and held it against the top of the pole so Hector could fix it in place with the glass knob.

Hector's heart soared. With Tumbleweed's help, he could make up all the time he'd lost. He stared out across the vast, dry desert. Nothing could stop him now.

CHAPTER NINETEEN

"There it is," Amber said as Kaal's walls came into view in front of them. Traveling with Dani, she'd covered the distance back to Kaal much faster than with the caravan.

Dani stopped Felicity and jumped up to stand on the seat, shading her eyes for a better view. "That's strange. There's some kind of giant man breaking through the city walls. I think Kaal must be under attack." Her voice cracked with fear, and Amber guessed it would be a long time before Dani got over what had happened to her family.

"Don't worry," Amber said, patting her leg. "That's just the Bronze Giant. My friend and I got it working, and it crashed into the wall. But it won't hurt anyone now. Only he and I know how to make it go."

Dani dropped back down to sit on the bench. "I see why you worried he might be in trouble. I bet the folks in the city didn't like that too much."

"Yeah, but that's not what got him banished from

Kaal. It's his lightning machine and those knights I'm worried about."

"Lightning machine?" Dani's hands tightened on the reins. Felicity felt the tension and stamped his foot. "Your friend is this Hector guy?" She frowned and glanced out into the desert away from the city.

"Yes, of course. But those knights don't understand. They think he's made a weapon, but it's not. It's something far better, far more valuable."

"I can imagine," Dani whispered. "Very, very valuable. I thought it might be when the knights rode off so quickly."

Amber waited for Dani to get Felicity moving, but Dani just sat there, staring out into the desert and chewing her lip. When she spoke, her voice was ragged as if trying to hold back tears. "I suppose when we get to the city, we'll have to split up. I have something I have to do. Something very important that takes me on past Kaal, but . . . you've been nice to me. I—" She squeezed her eyes closed and turned away. Twitching the reins, she got Felicity moving.

"Maybe when you're done, we'll see each other again," Amber said. She felt sorry for her new friend.

"No. I don't think we will," Dani said with just a touch of bitterness to her voice. "I'm glad I got to know you though, Amber. Most people aren't like you. Most people do whatever they must to take care of themselves. Whatever it takes to survive and make a decent life. Hector's lucky to have a friend like you."

Amber rubbed Dani's scarred arm. "I'm your friend too. Always remember that, all right?"

Dani gave Amber a sad smile and urged Felicity into a canter. Before long, they reached the city gates and passed inside. Buildings crowded up around them, and dozens of people in the street hindered their progress. Dani stopped just inside the gate.

"I guess this is it," Dani said. "You go your way. I go mine." She gave Amber a tight hug and lifted her down from the wagon.

"Good-bye," Amber whispered, then turned and ran along the street to the section of town where she and Hector had shared the lab. She reached it just after noon and sighed in contentment as she stepped inside out of the heat. The aroma of acid and copper still lingered in the empty room.

Amber walked around the table and uncovered the sender-receiver device that waited against the back wall. She pulled the lever that lowered Hector's zinc and copper stacks into the acid. The lightning eased into the wire, ready for her to use it. She pressed a handle, which made a *click-clicking* sound beneath her fingers, but nothing else happened. She waited.

Still nothing.

Groaning, she shut the device down. She figured Hector should have reached the dwarf kingdom by now. It had already been weeks. But no response from Hector could only mean one thing—something had gone wrong.

Amber covered the machine again and raced from the lab, her heart pounding. She dodged crowds of people as she ran down the street to the city's back wall, weaving through their legs and climbing over carts or any other obstacles that got in her way. Shouts of annoyance followed her progress. She ignored them and kept going, straight to the steps that led up the back wall.

One of the city guards on the wall tried to stop her, but she ducked under his arms and ran past. She kept going until she reached the point where Hector's underground wire came out under the wall and up into the desert.

Her first fear was that somehow the wire had been dug up or cut. Hector had been sure that the people of the city would be too afraid of the lightning to bother it, but he could have been wrong.

She squinted at the wire below. He'd attached it to a pole and then strung it out into the desert. The copper wire glittered in the sunlight, untouched. The hoof prints of the knights' horses marred the ground alongside it.

A shadow moved next to the wall, and Amber glanced over. Her jaw dropped. Felicity cantered up, pulling Dani and her little house wagon. When Dani reached the wire, she turned and followed it out into the desert.

Amber blinked, trying to grasp what it might mean. Dani's box house swayed back and forth with the motion of the wagon, its roof so tall it reached above Hector's wire. The sight of it brought a shocking thought to Amber.

Her trap outside the Goodlunds' bedroom window had been about that high. Standing on the back of the wagon, Dani would have been able to open the window without setting off the trap. And Dani was strong enough that she could toss the fabric right out onto the top of the wagon house in no time at all. Felicity was trained well enough to stand still for it, and go again with just a motion of Dani's hands.

Amber remembered seeing burlap bags inside Dani's house. They must have been the ones Dani used to muffle Felicity's steps. And Dani could have used a piece of the bearskin to make Syndall believe the thief had a beard. She'd left the handkerchief behind in the shop on purpose. But where was the stolen fabric? Amber stared at the wagon house as it retreated along the wire. She'd been inside with Dani and never seen any sign of the material.

A thought came to Amber, and she slapped the side of her head in frustration. She'd been so blind. The bottom of the wagon was a good foot lower than the floor inside the house. Dani had a secret compartment.

Dani and her wagon sped out along the copper wire, fast and silent.

Amber felt sick and more afraid for Hector than ever. Dani had stolen the Goodlunds' material. Now she was going after Hector's device. Very valuable, Dani had said, and it was true. Sold to the right people, Hector's invention could bring enough steel to buy a mansion and beautiful things and allow Dani to live like royalty for the rest of her life.

Amber shook her head in dismay. The right people—not the knights, not the dwarves, but others who would love the power to conquer every city and village on the continent—would pay so much.

Chapter Twenty

Using his wire cutters, Hector spliced a section of the insulation-coated wire onto the end of the longer piece. Above him, red and orange spires marked Tumbleweed's hidden lair.

The dragon pranced around Hector as he worked, miraculously not tripping over the wire and knocking down the last pole they'd set up. "I get Hector's invention. I get Hector's invention."

Hector laughed. "Well, not yet. This is just the wire. I'll have to build another sender-receiver device to put in the Grand Conversation Hall. First we have to finish stringing the wire to Goldmane's kingdom, all right?"

Tumbleweed blew out an affirmative lick of flame.

"Let's go inside then," Hector said.

Tumbleweed lifted him up, flapped his wings to rise into the air, then dived into the sand. Even with Tumbleweed pointing it out to him, Hector had not been able to see the entrance to the lair—too much sand, a perfect camouflage.

He let the wire slip out between his fingers as Tumbleweed carried him through the sand-covered entry into the lair.

In no time he had the wire strung down the passageway to the Grand Conversation Hall, then out through a different passage and aboveground once more.

He hoped this little detour to Tumbleweed's lair hadn't used up so much of the wire it wouldn't be able to stretch all the way to the Dargaard Mountains. Still, it was worth it just to see the delight in Tumbleweed's eyes.

Even with the dragon's help, it had taken them days to reach the lair. They stayed that night, restocking the food and water supplies in the wagon and talking in front of the giant fireplace.

Tumbleweed stroked one of the statues as he spoke to Hector. "I think my parents would have liked you."

"I'm sure my father would like you too," Hector said. "Maybe someday you could come to Haggersmoore and meet him."

"I'd like that." Tumbleweed settled down in front of the fire and stared at the dancing flames.

Hector woke early the next morning, anxious to get going again. Bit by bit, pole by pole, he and Tumbleweed strung the wire past the sandstone pillars and cliffs that marked the desert's edge. Just before nightfall, they climbed a steep rise to a plateau and found an ocean of flat grassland waving in front of them.

Tumbleweed's eyes grew wide. He let go of the harness and charged out into the grass, pawing and sniffing and cavorting.

"So much green," he sang. "Look at it all. Green, green, green everywhere. And what's that over there?" He took to the air and zipped away.

Hector shook his head and made camp for the night. He'd never seen anyone so delighted by a simple patch of grassland. But he supposed it made sense, since Tumbleweed had never been out of the desert before.

A few minutes later Tumbleweed returned. "It's water," he roared. "A big, wide snake of water that goes on and on in both directions. So much water! I can't believe it. Just running along out in the open and everything."

"It's just a river," Hector said. "Tomorrow we'll have to get across it. See those black bumps in the distance? Those are the mountains. If you think the grasslands are green, wait until you see the forest."

"Forest?" Tumbleweed hopped over the fire that Hector was trying to start. The rush of wind from his wings blew out the sparks from Hector's flint and steel.

"Do you mind?" Hector said. "I'm trying to cook dinner here."

"Silly gnome." Tumbleweed bent down over the small pile of wood and blew out a lick of flame, igniting it. "If you want fire, all you have to do is ask."

The next day, the river proved to be somewhat of a challenge. Tumbleweed could fly back and forth over it easily. He could even carry Hector. They got a pole set up on either side, but then it came time to move the wagon.

Tumbleweed hovered in the air above it, then grabbed it with all four claws while Hector stood in the back to let out the wire. But when Tumbleweed tried to lift it from the ground, it tipped, throwing Hector out and tangling the rope and the poles with the other supplies.

Hector hit the ground on his stomach and rolled onto his side, gasping for air. "Put it down," he tried to say, but the words barely came out as a whisper.

Supplies trailed down on the grass behind Tumbleweed as he managed to carry it a few yards and then slumped to the ground next to the riverbank.

"I can't," he huffed. "It's just too heavy and awkward."

Hector climbed to his feet and stumbled over to the young dragon. He rubbed Tumbleweed's skull plate. "It's all right. Give me a minute. I'll think of something."

He stared across the blue expanse of the Vingaard

River. A dozen different inventions for crossing flashed through his mind. In the end he chose the easiest course of action. It might take a while, but certainly not as long as going for supplies to build a giant lifting arm or automatic paddle boat—or laying line further southwest to cross at the nearest ferry down by Kentrell.

Going back to the wagon, he roused the disconsolate dragon, then sent him about carrying the supplies across a little bit at a time—first the lightning machine with its sender-receiver device, then the poles, followed by the food and water, the ladder, tools, and equipment.

"Now the coil of wire," Hector said, motioning for Tumbleweed to lift the coil into the air. "Be careful. Let it out slowly as you cross so you don't uproot the pole."

Tumbleweed rumbled an acknowledgment. With a few flaps of his wings, he got the wire across and set it gently next to the rest of the supplies. That just left the wagon. Now empty of all its cargo, Hector had Tumbleweed pull it into the water and guide it while it floated across.

The river crossing took most of the morning, but they made better progress in the afternoon. The mountains grew bigger on the horizon, and Tumbleweed became more excited. "I want to see trees. Can't I fly ahead?"

Hector stared at the distant mountains. They'd reach them by nightfall the next night. But getting to the mountains wasn't the biggest problem now. They still faced the one thing he'd procrastinated worrying about. Getting across the desert had seemed like a big enough task by itself. But what lay ahead in the mountains had him stumped.

"What's wrong?" Tumbleweed asked, sensing his worry. "Why don't you want me to fly up there? I can do it while you're sleeping."

"You flying over there isn't the problem. The problem is I don't know where the dwarf kingdom is and how to find it."

"How can you not know where a whole kingdom is?" Tumbleweed asked.

Hector spluttered for an answer.

"Well, don't worry. I'll just fly around the mountains until I find it. It can't be that hard to see them," Tumbleweed said.

Hector grimaced and waved for Tumbleweed to stop talking for a moment. "The dwarf kingdom is underground. They hide the entrances—like your lair. No one can get in who doesn't belong there."

Tumbleweed let out a deep rumble and paced around Hector. "You're saying you planned this grand scheme to take your device to the dwarves, and you don't even know where they are?"

Hector flinched away from the dragon's accusing voice. "It's not *that* silly. I mean, I have met the dwarf prince,

Goldmane. He knows me. If I can just find him, I'm sure he'll listen to me about the device."

Tumbleweed rolled his eyes, flapped his wings, and lifted into the air. "You get some rest. I'm going to scout out the mountains and see if I can find any dwarves. Maybe I'll catch a few above ground."

Hector watched him fly off across the grasslands to the dark hills in the distance. "First put up the line. Then find the dwarves," he muttered, rubbing his head. "One thing at a time. It will all work out." He hoped. He'd already been through so much to get to this point. If he couldn't find the dwarves, or they wouldn't listen to him, all his work would be in vain.

Chapter Twenty-One

Two days later, Kyani skimmed the ocean of green below him, still looking for the dwarves while Hector strung the last of the wire across the hills. Leaves whispered in the wind of the dragon's passing. The scent of moisture and life rose up from the forest, and the rich aroma intoxicated him.

So many trees. Amazing.

But he'd found no sign of the dwarves, just sheer rock or foliage so dense he couldn't see the ground. His wings grew tired from his long flight, and he searched for a place to land. There. An opening in the trees. He folded his wings and dropped to the fern-covered ground.

A spray of dew lifted around him as he touched down.

The small crystalline drops of water surprised him, and he turned this way and that, flicking out his tongue, trying to catch them before they fell. Soon the glistening water covered his chest and legs.

"Oh, Hector," he rumbled with delight, settling

down into the dewy ferns and filling his stomach. "You should see this. I never dreamed there could be so many dew drops."

He foraged deeper into the trees' shadows, sniffing at branches and clawing at piles of moldering leaves. Beetles and ants swarmed along a rotting log. "Hey, what's the rush?" he said to the scurrying creatures. He put his claw down in their midst and let the little black ants crawl along his talons. "It's a lovely forest you have here. Mind if I stay? Lots of food. Lots of everything." He smiled, shook off the ants, and ambled on.

His way grew darker. He shivered. "It would be nice if you'd let a little sunlight in," he told a towering tree that spread its canopy high overhead.

In the desert he'd always had plenty of sunlight to warm him. Not here. He shivered again and searched the canopy for a hole big enough to fly through. He'd left the little clearing behind. Tree branches tangled together above him. Clinging vines wrapped the branches and spread out, blocking the sky. Everything around him was wet, green, and dark.

Growling, Kyani turned back, retracing his wandering path. Only his own faint scent on the plants told him which way he'd come. Little black birds flocked in the tree branches, chattering at him.

He snuffed at them and asked if they knew the way back to the clearing. They took to the air, screaming. Their little bodies lifted between the thick branches to the sky. But there was no way he could follow them.

A new scent came to him, earthy and strong. It's the dwarves, he thought. Must be. It didn't smell like any of the other animals he'd smelled yet. The scent crossed his own path twice, and then vanished.

He turned back to try and find it again.

A snarl sounded from the bushes, and a large black creature lunged out and sank its sharp teeth into Kyani's tender wing membrane.

Kyani bellowed and grabbed the creature, squeezing it until it yelped and let go. He tossed it far into the trees, but three others sprang out, one on each side and one on his flank. They attacked.

Kyani lifted his wings out of the way, and their jaws scraped against his scales. They growled and barked and came at him again and again. Frightened, Kyani filled the air with his sleep gas. His three attackers wavered, then sank to the ground, snoring. The one he'd thrown aside, out of range of the gas, staggered to its feet. It lifted its head and let out a long plaintive howl. Other howls answered.

The forest came alive with shaggy four-legged bodies. Kyani whipped around, trying to fight back one then another of them, only to have a half dozen more attack from his flanks. He tried to breathe his sleep gas on them, but he had none left. It would take time for his body to make more.

One of them scrambled up his tail onto his back and tore at his raised wings. It had figured out it could do little damage against his scales.

The others caught on and leaped up, biting and tearing.

Kyani roared in outrage and pain. The thick forest deadened his cry.

Giving up on trying to stop his attackers without hurting them, he sucked in a hot breath and sent a jet of fire over his shoulder at the ones on his back. The smell of burned fur and flesh filled the air, and the creatures tumbled off of him.

The others backed away, circling. Waiting.

A new one stepped out from between the trees. It was twice as big as the others. Its mottled gray fur covered bulging muscles and a deep chest from which came a growl so ferocious and angry that Kyani backed away.

"What do you want?" Kyani said. "You're not dwarves, I guess. Hector said dwarves walk on two feet. What are you, and why are you trying to hurt me? I mean you no harm."

The big gray growled again, and the others slunk back into the bushes, but they weren't gone. Kyani could still smell and hear them hunched down close by, but the trees and plants crowded him, blocking his view and hiding his tormentors—not like out in the desert, where he could see forever and know danger approached long before it reached him.

The gray watched him with burning yellow eyes.

"Do you speak?" Kyani asked it. "Can we talk this out? I just want to leave now."

He took a step, and the whole pack burst from the leaves at once. They jumped on him, catching his wings and dragging them down to the ground. He roared in pain, and the leader dived at his throat, clamping its jaws around Kyani's neck.

Kyani tried to pull away, but they had him pinned. He couldn't move without shredding his wings. The jaws of the big gray were cutting off his air.

He couldn't breathe. The edges of his vision became clouded and gray. He sensed more rustling in the underbrush. More creatures come to finish him off.

"Shoot!" a gruff voice said.

Small sharp sticks with feathers on the end flew out of the trees and sank into the creatures that held Kyani. Were those arrows? Kyani wondered. His father had told him humans used arrows to fight. Three of his attackers fell to the arrows, whimpering and flopping to the ground.

More arrows followed the first set a heartbeat later. Four more of his attackers died. The creature at his throat, though hit by an arrow, kept its grip, squeezing ever tighter.

Kyani's lungs screamed for air. He grew dizzy and slumped to the ground.

The deep voice he'd heard before uttered a string of curses, and a golden-haired man rushed from the trees. Well, maybe not a man. He was too short for that, though a bit taller and much broader than Hector. He had a lush, full beard the same color as his hair, and he swung a heavy axe right through the big gray's body. Its jaws fell away from Kyani's neck, and Kyani gasped for breath.

His remaining attackers howled and fled, but from the sounds of chopping amid the leaves and the dying whimpers from the creatures, Kyani guessed they didn't get far. The golden-haired person and his friends took care of that.

Kyani winced at the sound of the dying creatures. "What are they?"

The golden-haired man kicked the gray creature's body away from Kyani. "They're worgs, enemies of my kingdom. The real question is, what are you?" He ran his hand down Kyani's neck. "I've never seen a lizard quite your size before and certainly not in the mountains. I saw some pretty big lizards out in that blasted desert, but we're a long way from there."

Kyani shuddered, then stood and raised his bleeding wings. "You think I'm a lizard?"

His rescuer gasped and stepped back to stare at him.

Another short man pushed his way out of the under-brush, this one older with a grizzled gray beard. "It's a dragon, Your Highness," he said in awe. "A brass dragon from the looks of it. But very young."

"Blasted worgs." A third man joined the other two, and in a moment a half dozen of them stood around Kyani.

The golden-haired one bowed. "I am Goldmane, prince of the dwarves of the Northern Dargaard Mountains. Welcome to my kingdom."

CHAPTER TWENTY-TWO

Hector put his ladder up next to a tall oak tree. He bit his lip as he affixed his last glass knob and hooked the copper wire to the tree.

This was it. The end of the line.

He had only enough wire left to string down to his sender-receiver device.

He scanned the sky above the mountains, looking for Tumbleweed. His gut hurt from worrying about his friend. Tumbleweed had flown off early that morning in search of the dwarves again and not returned.

Now the sun stood high in the sky on the day Hector had written on the envelope for Shem. Hector was out of wire, and out of time. No dwarves and no Tumbleweed.

Hector slid down the ladder and fixed the end of the wire to his device. Then he pulled the lever to power it up. Lightning sang through the machine and waited. Hector pressed his sender button, tapping out the code that sent short bursts of lightning along the copper wire where the receiver on the other end would write out the dots for Shem to decipher from the code book.

Hector waited for a response. The stick of charcoal on his own receiver device remained unmoving as minutes dragged by. Hector frowned and paced around the machine, rubbing his head. "It works. I know it works. It has to work." He stared at the silent device.

A wolf howl sounded in the distance, answered by a whole pack. Their eerie voices echoed among the mountain peaks. Hector shivered. He'd hate to have to fight off a wolf pack. From the sounds of their cries though, they seemed to be attacking something else at the moment.

Tumbleweed.

Hector left his device and ran toward the sound. A wolf pack would have no chance against an adult brass dragon, but Tumbleweed would likely try to talk with them, never realizing the danger until too late.

Hector raced up a steep incline, pushing aside tree branches and leaping over rocks that blocked his path. He wished he had his repeating crossbow, but he'd lost that long ago. He searched around in his apron for some other tool he could use as a weapon.

The trees gave way, and Hector skidded to a stop at the top of a steep cliff. Sheer gray rock plunged down for hundreds of feet below him.

The wolf howls ended, leaving the mountains silent

except for the moan of the wind rushing up from the rocks below.

Hector stared off across the jagged peaks that rose up one after another along the mountain range. He strained to hear any other sound or catch the glint of brass scales winging above the trees. Nothing.

"Tumbleweed!" he yelled. "Tumbleweed!" Only his own voice came echoing back to him.

Frowning, Hector traversed the edge of the cliff, looking for a way down.

The sharp *click* of the receiver arm filled the empty lab. Amber looked up blearily from the worktable where she'd dozed while waiting, hoping Hector was all right and that he'd send word via his device. She'd been waiting so long, she thought for a moment she was just imagining the sound.

When she came fully awake and realized what was happening, she jumped to her feet and leaned over the machine, watching as the receiver traced each dot and line on the paper.

Her hands fumbled for the code book.

The receiver went silent. Amber tore off the paper and sat down at the workbench to decipher the code.

Testing. Testing. Is anyone there receiving?

"Yes!" she shouted. "Yes, Hector. I'm here."

"So it seems," Shem said, stepping into the room along with Peyote and several more of the city guard. "But why are you here? And what is that horrible machine still doing in my city?" He waved a letter with Hector's handwriting on it. "I told Hector to get out and take his invention with him."

"But he did leave," Amber protested. "And he took the one that shocked you with him. This is a different one."

"Looks the same to me," Shem said, glaring at the sender-receiver.

Amber backed away from him.

He blew out a deep breath and softened his voice. "I'm sorry, Amber. I don't mean to shout. It's just that Hector's invention is dangerous. I don't want anyone here getting hurt. You understand that, don't you?"

Amber nodded. "But Hector has it working on the other end now. He's going to have Goldmane send a message to you." She held up the paper. "You see, it works. We can talk to the dwarves in the mountains instantaneously. I just need to send him an answer so he knows we're ready to receive it here."

"You'll do no such thing! Don't you dare power up that invention. Come out now. Come away," Shem ordered.

"No," Amber said. "I have to stay. I need to warn Hector about the thief and the knights that want his invention."

Shem motioned to his guards. They grabbed Amber and carried her outside, then locked the door and took up position on either side. "No one goes in or out," Shem said, "until I get Amber here to tell me how to dismantle that thing safely."

"I'll never tell you anything!" Amber shouted.

"We'll see about that." Shem hoisted her under his arm and strode down the street to the city jail. He set her down gently in one of the cells. "Think it over," he said. "This is for the safety of the whole city. I'll come back in a few hours and have a little chat with you."

Shem walked out, and Amber plopped down on the straw mattress against the wall.

"A few hours," she muttered. That should be plenty of time to think of an invention to get her out of there and back into the lab to send a message to Hector. A little jail cell wouldn't stop her from warning him about the thief.

CHAPTER TWENTY-THREE

Hector's muscles burned as he felt along the gray rock for another handhold. His cheek stung from where he'd scraped it against the stone. The salty taste of his dripping sweat filled his mouth. Clinging to the side of the cliff, he couldn't spare a hand to wipe it away.

He worked his fingers into a crevice and adjusted his position, moving downward inch by inch. Finally his feet touched ground at the cliff's bottom. He slumped down, gasping for breath. It had taken him an hour to descend the cliff, and he'd heard no further sound from the wolves the whole time.

He squinted, searching the hills for any sign of Tumbleweed. He's a dragon, Hector tried to reassure himself. Wolves couldn't bite through his scales. If they attacked, he'd burn them all to ashes. The thought didn't ease the rock in the pit of Hector's stomach.

He got up and brushed himself off. Tumbleweed could be in trouble, and Hector would do whatever he must to find him.

A rumble filled the air, and the mountain shook, knocking Hector to the ground. The sound grew deeper. It was coming from the cliff face he'd just climbed down.

The gray rock cracked in a circle and pushed out like a giant cork coming out of a bottle. Hector dodged just in time to keep it from squishing him as it separated from the rest of the cliff face and rolled aside, revealing a dark cave beyond.

The ground stopped shaking, and a half dozen dwarves stepped out. The sun cast its rays on the lead dwarf's golden hair.

"Goldmane!" Hector scrambled to his feet. "I'm so glad to see you." He thought of Shem and his sender-receiver device—the chance to prove that his invention worked.

Then he thought of Tumbleweed, lost in the mountains somewhere, hurt, maybe dying. "You won't believe this, but I've lost my dragon. I think he's hurt. You know these mountains better than anyone. Will you help me find him?"

Goldmane laughed.

"No, it's true," Hector said. "A brass dragon. He's my friend, but he's just a youngling."

Goldmane held up his hand to silence Hector. "I'll tell you what. Let's make a deal. We'll return your friend to you on one condition."

"What? I'll do anything to save him."

Goldmane shook his head. "All I want you to do is get

him to shut up. If I have to listen to him babble any longer I'll go crazy."

"Good afternoon, Hector. Look what I found," Tumbleweed's voice rumbled from inside the cave. "Dwarves." Hector looked away from Goldmane and saw Tumbleweed lumber out into the sunshine. He spread his wings to soak in the light, and Hector noticed the edges were torn in several places.

"Tumbleweed!" Hector shouted and raced over to him. "I've been so worried about you." He wrapped his arms around the dragon's foreleg and gave him a tight hug. "What happened to your wings? I heard wolves."

"Worgs, actually," Goldmane said, a deadly glint in his eyes. "But we took care of them. Filthy creatures. They should know better than to come into my kingdom."

"Worgs." Hector shuddered and reached up to pat Tumbleweed's smooth scales. "Come back to the wagon. I'll put some salve on those wings."

Tumbleweed folded his wings against his back. "Goldmane's men already tended to them. I have to tell you, dwarf salve stings like crazy, but I think it's helping. Besides, there's something more important to do first. You need to show Prince Goldmane your device."

The device. He'd forgotten about it for a moment in his excitement to see Tumbleweed. "Your Highness, please come this way," Hector said to Goldmane, then stopped. The cliff now stood between him and the sender-receiver.

Goldmane rubbed his beard. "We've returned your dragon. Isn't that enough?"

"Yes. Thank you. But I have something I think you'll like. It's a communication device that will allow you to talk to the people of Kaal without even having to travel there. You see, I've made this lightning machine, which I have hooked to a sender-receiver. The sender sends a message via the lightning out to Kaal where there is a receiver that writes it down. Then they can look up the stuff in the code book and see what you said and send a response. It all happens as fast as lightning. *Bam*! They have your words. *Bam* again. They answer you back. Except we have to get up this cliff because I left it over on the other side of the hill when I heard the worgs howl."

"Hold on. Slow down. You're talking too fast," Goldmane said. "I don't understand."

Hector took a deep breath. He'd forgotten dwarves were just as slow as humans. He repeated his message, taking time to separate each word and pause for a second between sentences.

Goldmane scratched his head. "You're saying I can talk to Shem in Kaal instantly, without going anywhere or sending a messenger?"

"Right." Hector jumped up and down and clapped with delight.

The other dwarves snickered. Goldmane waved for them to be silent. "And you think it actually works?"

Hector nodded, his excitement seeping away. "I know it isn't good form to have an invention work right. My father and I are always in trouble with the other gnomes about that. They think there's something wrong with us. But I'm telling you, my sender-receiver does work. Come and see for yourself."

Goldmane smiled, and the other dwarves broke out into deep, hearty laughter.

Tumbleweed growled and caught the nearest dwarf in his claw, lifting him up to look him straight in the eyes. "Stop laughing. Hector almost died trying to set up this device for you. Show a little respect."

Hector motioned for Tumbleweed to set the dwarf down. The dragon complied.

"Well," Goldmane said, stroking his beard. "I guess it couldn't hurt to take a look since it's so close."

"But the cliff." Hector's muscles still ached from climbing down it.

Goldmane laughed. "We'll just go inside and climb the stairs up to the next level. It shouldn't take long. Come on." Goldmane motioned Hector inside the mountain, and a few minutes later they all stood around his sender-receiver device.

Tumbleweed rumbled with pleasure. He tapped Goldmane's chest with a pointed talon. "Now watch. You'll see that it works." He nodded to Hector.

Hector powered up the device and sent another message to Kaal. *Shem, this is Goldmane. Can you hear me?* He hoped Shem had opened the letter by now and read the code book so he could tap out an answer.

Nothing happened.

"Well," Goldmane said. "Is that it?"

"Give him a moment," Hector said. "He doesn't have the code memorized. He'll have to look it up in the book to see what you said. But when he knows it, he'll be able to answer back right away."

"Right," Goldmane said. He walked over to the lightning machine and scrutinized the wires and zinc and copper stacks submerged in acid. "Sure does smell bad. What does this wire do?"

He reached out to touch the wire. Hector opened his mouth to shout a warning, but someone else spoke first.

"I wouldn't do that if I were you." A Solamnic Knight, wearing bright armor with a crown etched into his breastplate, rode out of the trees on a tall bay warhorse. His gray hair and insignia marked him as one of the highest-ranked leaders of the Knights of the Crown. He swung out of the saddle and crunched to the ground. Five other knights rode out after him.

"Sir Guyon," Hector said. A jolt went through him as if he'd been shocked by his lightning machine.

Goldmane stepped back from the invention.

"Hello, Hector," Sir Guyon said, walking over. "I guess the reports of your death were a bit inaccurate."

Hector backed away, positioning himself between Guyon and his invention.

"You know your father has been taking our steel for several years now, promising us the greatest weapon ever invented." Sir Guyon gave Hector a grim smile. "I was starting to doubt that he'd ever deliver, but then I heard about your lightning machine. I guess I shouldn't have doubted. It can kill a man with a single touch, I've heard."

"No, not kill. Well . . . yes, I guess. Maybe, depending on the man, what he's wearing, atmospheric conditions, and whether or not he's grounded. But, no! This isn't a weapon."

"Kill a man with a single touch?" Goldmane said, edging away from the lightning machine. "Are you sure?" he asked Sir Guyon.

"Absolutely." Guyon took another step toward Hector. The other knights dismounted, their hands on their sword hilts. "It almost killed the leader of Kaal. I talked to several witnesses."

"Well, well," Goldmane said, rubbing his hands together and smiling. "Now that sounds like something useful. I think this calls for a demonstration."

"No," Hector cried. "Don't touch it. I haven't got the wires safely coated yet."

"I have no intention of touching it myself," Gold-mane said, looking around. "Let's see. How about one of the horses?"

"No," Sir Guyon said sternly. "Keep your hands off our mounts. I don't need a demonstration here. We'll take it back to Palanthas and then see how it works so we can make more of them. Deactivate it, Hector. It's time to pay up."

Sir Guyon motioned to his men, and they surrounded the machine.

"Oh no, you don't," Goldmane said. The dwarves lifted their battle-axes off their backs and pushed forward. "The lightning weapon is ours. Hector just offered it to us, and I accept."

Chapter Twenty-Four

Now, wait a minute," Hector said as the knights and dwarves faced off with one another. "It's not a weapon. You don't need to fight. You can both use it to talk to each other. Don't you see?"

"It doesn't matter what you think it should do, Hector," Sir Guyon said, drawing his sword. "It can be used as a weapon, and we've already paid handsomely for it. You can't go giving it to these dwarves. What did they offer you, anyway?"

Hector looked to Tumbleweed for help. Tumbleweed shrugged. He'd tucked his wings close to his sides and backed into the trees when the knights arrived. "Well, nothing. It's not for sale. This is just a demonstration."

The smell of sweat and anger hung in the air. The leaves rustled in the breeze. Sir Guyon squared off with Goldmane. "Get out of my way, dwarf."

Hector licked his lips and spread his arms to protect the sender-receiver.

Guyon swung his sword. Goldmane blocked it with his axe. The metal clang rattled Hector's teeth. "Don't! Are you crazy?" he cried. "If your sword hits the wire—"

His voice was lost in the din of sudden battle. Knights and dwarves sprang at one another, swinging their weapons and shouting war cries.

Hector reached for the lever to shut off the lightning machine, but just as he did, the receiver clicked into motion. Lightning from the other end of the line spun around the coiled wire, creating a magnet that lifted one end of the receiver arm and pressed the other end with the charcoal stick against the paper. A ratchet spun the paper forward, and within a few seconds the receiver covered it with an array of dots and lines. All the while the dwarves and knights stayed locked in combat, oblivious to the miracle.

"I've done it!" Hector shouted. "See, it works. Look, look!"

No one heard him.

The machine fell silent, and he ripped the paper off, intending to read it. Sir Guyon's sword sang over the top of his head and buried itself into the device's wooden frame. Goldmane leaped forward and kicked Guyon in the chest, knocking him to the ground. He swung his axe at Guyon's head.

Sir Guyon twisted off the ground, grabbed his sword free from the device, and swung it at Goldmane.

Goldmane leaped to safety.

"Stop," Hector cried. "Look. I have a message."

"To the abyss with your message," Goldmane spat. "No snotty knight is going to come into my kingdom and start a fight without paying for it." He lifted his axe overhead and raced at Guyon.

Guyon dodged to the side and tripped him. Goldmane went down, but rolled back to his feet without stopping and swung a killing blow at Guyon's chest. Sir Guyon deflected it, forcing the axe into the guts of Hector's device.

As soon as the steel connected with the wire, an arc of lightning sprang across it down into Goldmane's arms and chest. His hair stood on end, and his clothes caught fire, but he remained frozen with the lightning's power, unable to pull the axe away from the wire.

Hector threw the lever, lifting the stacks from the acid and cutting off the lightning.

Goldmane's axe came free, and he slumped to the ground, still burning. Hector dived on top of the dwarf, smothering the flames. Goldmane lay limp beneath him.

The sounds of battle died, leaving the mountainside in stunned silence. Knights and dwarves gathered around the fallen prince.

Hector swallowed. The smell of burned clothes and skin made him nauseous. He looked into the dwarf's blackened face. Goldmane's beard was curled into a short stubble. A faint ember still lingered among the hairs. Hector pinched it out. Goldmane's eyes were closed, and he remained motionless.

"Get off." One of the dwarves lifted Hector from Goldmane and tossed him aside.

"Is he alive?" Sir Guyon asked.

An old dwarf with a gray beard leaned over his fallen prince. "He's breathing, faintly. Heart still beating. It will take more than a little lightning to kill a dwarf."

Hector heaved a sigh of relief. Sir Guyon grabbed him by the shoulders and lifted him into the air. "Not a weapon, eh?"

"I tried to warn you," Hector stuttered. "Not safe to fight next to."

Guyon snorted. "At least now we've had our little demonstration. I was right. It does work. Pack that thing up and get ready to go. We're taking it back to Palanthas."

The dwarves looked up darkly but were too concerned about Goldmane to protest. "We better get him inside to the healers," the old dwarf said.

The others agreed. They lifted Goldmane and headed for their cave.

Sir Guyon shook Hector and dropped him. "Get your device. Let's go."

Hector picked himself up from the ground. His head hurt, and he wondered how everything could have gone so wrong just at the moment when his device had performed so well. Sir Guyon and his knights had ruined everything. Anger welled up inside Hector. He folded his arms across his chest and glared at Guyon.

"No. You can't have it. I will destroy it before I ever see it used as a weapon again. I saw you knock Goldmane's axe into the wire. You did it on purpose."

Sir Guyon snorted. "Of course I did. It's just what the dwarf deserved. That weapon is ours." He nodded to his men, and one of them grabbed Hector, lifted him off the ground, and held him while another bound his arms and feet. "I'm afraid I can't let you destroy it, Hector. It's too valuable."

A deep rumble filled the air and burst forth in a deafening roar. "Release my friend!" Tumbleweed bellowed, charging out of the trees. "Or I'll burn you all far worse than that dwarf got."

He sucked in a deep breath and held it. Flames licked between his teeth.

The knights dropped Hector and backed away.

"A-a dragon!" One of the younger knights fumbled his sword, dropping it to the ground. "W-where did it come from?"

Tumbleweed breathed the fire into the sky over their heads. The heat sent rivulets of sweat down Hector's back.

"I've been here the whole time," Tumbleweed roared.

"You were just so bent on fighting you failed to notice. Stupid humans." He advanced on the knights.

Sir Guyon held his ground, looking Tumbleweed over. "He's just a baby," he murmured to the other knights. "Go get the lances."

The youngest two knights raced into the trees where they'd sent the horses.

Hector rolled to his knees. "No. Please."

His father had fought in the War of the Lance and told Hector all about the knights' dragonlances. They could take down a full-grown red dragon. Tumbleweed didn't have a chance. Why would a Solamnic Knight use a dragonlance on a good dragon? Couldn't they see that Tumbleweed was a Brass?

Hector couldn't let them kill Tumbleweed, but he was too small to stop them. There was only one way to save his friend. A sharp pain stabbed across his chest at the thought of it. It took all his will to force the words out of his mouth.

"I'll give you my invention. It's yours. Take it. Just leave Tumbleweed alone."

Hector held his breath.

A smug smile spread across Sir Guyon's face. "I'll take your offer, Hector."

The other knights came out of the trees, mounted, but without lances.

Hector stood and rubbed his head in confusion. "They don't have lances?"

Sir Guyon let out a mocking laugh. "You think we carry them with us everywhere? Besides, the metallic dragons are our allies. If we kill this wyrmling, we'll have to answer to all the others. It could start a war."

Hector's face burned. They wouldn't have killed Tumbleweed. He'd just given his device away for nothing.

"Hey, I'm not a wyrmling," Tumbleweed said. "I'm older than that . . . barely."

Sir Guyon stepped forward and cut the ropes binding Hector.

Hector jumped to his feet and raced over to Tumbleweed. Tumbleweed put a protective claw around him and pulled him up against his chest. Hector couldn't stop shaking.

"It's all right," Tumbleweed whispered in his ear. "I would have used my sleep gas on them. They couldn't hurt me."

Hector looked at Tumbleweed's torn wings and wondered if that was true. Was a pack of worgs more dangerous than trained Solamnic Knights?

"But hey," Tumbleweed said, his voice brightening, "your device worked. Didn't it? You've got the proof right in your hand. What does it say?"

Hector spread the paper he'd crumpled up in his fist during the fight. The dots and lines stared up at him. He didn't need his code book to read the cipher—he'd invented it, after all.

Sir Guyon stared at him. "What's that?"

"A message from Kaal," Hector said. "Like I tried to tell you. My invention is a communication device, not a weapon."

Guyon shook his head and stepped closer. "What does it say?"

The other knights gathered around. Tumbleweed growled a warning and gripped Hector tighter.

Hector cleared his throat and read aloud.

Hector,
Be careful. The knights are coming. Also a thief who plans to steal the invention and sell it. Please be safe.
Love,
Amber

Hector looked up from the page. His eyes met Guyon's then slid past him to the place where the copper wire came down from the tree to his device. Except the wire had been snipped, and the device had vanished.

Chapter Twenty-Five

It's gone." Hector tore loose from Tumbleweed's grasp and raced over to the spot where his invention had been sitting during the battle. "It was here. Right here. You all saw it shock Goldmane." He looked around wildly for any sign of the device.

"The dwarves," the youngest knight said, sprinting to the cave, which thundered closed before he could reach it.

"It wasn't the dwarves," Guyon chided the younger knight. "Let me see that." He snatched the paper out of Hector's hands and held it up to read. "What? This is nothing more than scribbles."

"It's a code," Hector said, scanning the forest for any sign of the thief. Thick trees obstructed his vision. "Come on. The thief couldn't have gotten far." They'd only been distracted for a moment while tying Hector up and facing off with Tumbleweed.

"Mount up," Sir Guyon called to his men. "The thief

would have to have a wagon to carry that thing. We should be able to catch him."

The knights raced to their horses and galloped away, spreading out to look for any sign of the thief's trail.

Hector stared at the nub of the wire still dangling from the tree and rubbed his head. "A thief. Wants to sell it. Where would he go?"

"To a city," Tumbleweed blurted out. "My father always went to cities when he wanted stuff. He says you can get anything in Palanthas. It's huge."

Hector frowned, walked over to his wagon, and rummaged around for his map. "Palanthas is too far away." He knelt and spread the map out on the ground. "Here we are in the Dargaard Mountains. The closest city is Kalaman. That's just up the river to the bay. Maybe thirty miles."

Hector looked up at Tumbleweed. Scabs crusted the torn edges of his wings. It hurt Hector just to look at the wounds the worgs had inflicted. He winced. "Do you think you can fly?"

Tumbleweed rippled his wings and flapped them a few times. He lifted a foot off the ground, and his face contorted in pain. He dropped back down and shook his head. "The salve is helping. I can feel it. But I can't fly. Not yet." He hung his head.

Hector rolled up the map and shoved it into a pack

along with other supplies they'd need. "Then I guess we walk. Come on."

He set off down the mountain, but a scrap of paper caught on a bush stopped him. It was Amber's message, dropped by Sir Guyon in his hurry to go after the thief. Hector picked up the paper and stared at the marks, reading the message over again. The final line made his heart race: *Love, Amber.*

Amber had gone back to Kaal and waited for him to set up the device. She'd tried to warn him. He wondered what it had cost her. She'd wanted to go home so much, but she'd turned back to help him. Tears stung his eyes, and he folded the paper and slipped it into his apron.

"I love you too, Amber," he whispered.

He walked down the mountain with Tumbleweed beside him. Overhead his copper wire swayed in the breeze. He'd come so far in pursuit of his Life Quest. And the invention had worked. If only he'd read the message when it first came through, he might have kept it from being stolen.

I've failed you again, Amber, he thought. But when I see you again, I promise I'll listen to you.

"Do you suppose Shem was there?" he said out loud to Tumbleweed. "When I sent the message, I mean. Do you think he saw it and believes in my invention now?"

Tumbleweed had been strangely quiet as they walked.

He touched Hector's back with a gentle claw. "Does it matter what Shem thinks? You know your invention works, and I know your invention works. Isn't that enough? Does your Life Quest demand that other people acknowledge it or just that you accomplish it?"

Hector stared hard at the rocks and dirt beneath his feet. Here and there a tree root stuck up out of the ground. He stepped over one and paused. Tumbleweed's questions swam through his mind. Does it matter?

Of course his Life Quest mattered. Without a Life Quest a gnome would have no reason to keep on living and inventing. He'd known from the time he was a small child that he was destined to improve communication. He'd joined the Communication Guild early in life, before getting caught up in his father's work, making weapons. They'd kicked him out of the guild when he'd perfected his repeating crossbow.

If Shem had seen his sender-receiver work, if Hector had managed to set up communication between Kaal and Goldmane's kingdom, the other gnomes would have to let him back in the guild.

He pictured himself leading the guild some day. A great gnome. The inventor of the most amazing communication device ever: his sender-receiver. His lightning machine.

But it wasn't his anymore. The thief had taken it. Even if he and Tumbleweed caught the thief, the knights would come for it, and he'd have to give it to them. He'd promised it to them in exchange for Tumbleweed's life.

The knights would take it and use it as a weapon. The other gnomes would never let him back in the guild. He shook his head and clenched his fists in frustration.

"Don't be sad," Tumbleweed said. "We'll find the thief and get your invention back. I'm sure Shem saw that it worked. How could he not?"

Hector shoved his hands in his pockets and fingered Amber's message. *Love, Amber.* He'd failed in his communication with her. His time with Tumbleweed had taught him that. It did no good to keep talking and never listen. It was useless sending a message down the wire if no one was on the other end to receive it and answer back.

Maybe communication over a greater distance wasn't the answer. Maybe communicating better face-to-face was. What about that? The Communication Guild had never worked that angle before.

He and Tumbleweed reached the base of the mountain. In the distance they could see the knights galloping toward Kalaman. Tumbleweed started to follow them.

Hector stopped and stared back along his wire, reaching across the grassland, over the river, and through the desert to Kaal where Amber had heard his message and responded. *Love, Amber.*

"Tumbleweed," he called. "Let the knights have it. I already said I'd give it to them anyway. So what if they take it and use it as a weapon? I think my Life Quest is calling me another way. I have some serious communicating left to do in Kaal."

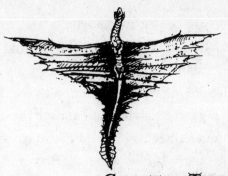

Chapter Twenty-Six

Amber closed the cell door and walked over to the lumpy bed in the room. Outside the thin slit of a window, the sky darkened. She'd been back to their lab twice since she'd sent the message warning Hector about the thief. Shem didn't know that, of course. As far as he was concerned, she was locked up in jail and would stay that way until she told him how to destroy Hector's invention. She'd refused, of course. Now she waited and worried.

No word from Hector. Nothing.

Perhaps she'd sent the message too late, and the knights had already reached him, or the thief had.

She fingered her bracelet, letting the hummingbird charms slide between her fingers. Their soft tinkling made her heart ache. She'd have to sneak out again in the morning. Maybe by then he'd send an answer and let her know all was well.

Hector stopped on the riverbank and scratched his bald head as he stared out across the rushing water. "Do you think you can swim across?" he asked Tumbleweed.

It had taken them two days to get back down out of the mountains and cross the grasslands to the river. Hector hadn't felt much like talking, and they'd passed the time and distance with Tumbleweed sharing stories of great dragons that his father had taught him.

Tumbleweed put a claw in the river and pulled it back out. "Too cold." He shivered. "I can't wait to get back to the desert. I've decided I like the warm sun better than all the dew in the mountains."

Hector smiled at the thought of Tumbleweed stretched out on the sand, soaking up the sunlight. But to get to the desert, they had to cross the river. It had been easy enough when Tumbleweed could fly, but the dragon's wings hadn't healed yet.

"I think I can climb up the post and go hand over hand across the wire," Hector said, pointing to where they'd strung the copper wire across the river. "But that won't work for you."

Growling, Tumbleweed paced back and forth along the river's edge. "Fly or swim. Fly or swim." He spread out his wings and gave them a little flap. "Ooouch!" He folded them against his sides. "Too bad I can't cross on the wire like you."

Hector laughed at the picture of Tumbleweed clinging to the wire.

"It's not funny," Tumbleweed huffed.

"Sorry," Hector said. "What do you want to do?"

Tumbleweed growled and went back to pacing. After a minute, he let out a giant snort and backed several yards away from the edge. Then he spread his wings and barreled at the water. Just as his feet touched the last bit of ground before the river, he jumped. The force of his spring carried him up and out across the water. His wings caught the air. He yelped in pain but kept them extended while he glided to the far bank.

"You did it!" Hector shouted as Tumbleweed landed on the soft grass on the other side. "Now my turn."

He climbed the pole, swung across on the wire, and touched down on the far side. Tumbleweed lay in the grass, flicking out his tongue to catch the morning dew drops.

"You all right?" Hector asked.

"My wings hurt. I need to rest for a few minutes."

Hector sat down next to Tumbleweed and leaned back against his smooth brass scales. "I guess this is as good a time as any for breakfast."

While he ate the last of his supplies, Hector watched the water race down the river. The currents twisted and eddied around the bushes and willows that crowded its banks downriver from Hector's poles. Something bumped and sloshed, caught in the many branches. At first Hector thought it was nothing more than a fallen log, but the more he looked at it, the more it looked like a flat wood plank.

Setting aside his pack and food, he walked downriver and pushed his way past the thick willows. There, tied up to the trees in a hidden cove, was a ferry. Hector stared at it, blinking in surprise. It was big enough to carry a horse and wagon across the river. It could have carried his wagon over the first time and Tumbleweed back.

He stepped out onto the sturdy flat boat. His foot slipped, and he fell on his backside in a pile of fresh horse droppings. He pinched his nose to ward off the smell and brushed the green goo from his pants.

Complaining about his rotten luck, he headed back to Tumbleweed, but stopped.

Fresh horse droppings? Someone had used the ferry that very morning, crossing the river in the same direction he and Tumbleweed were headed. But that was nowhere, just out into the desert. Couldn't be the knights. He'd seen them going northeast toward Kalaman. No merchants had any reason to travel this forgotten stretch of land.

Hector backtracked to the river's edge and examined the muddy bank. A set of wagon wheel ruts stretched from the ferry up the bank and then faded out into the grassland.

"Tumbleweed," Hector called. "You won't believe this. I think I've found the thief's tracks, and he's not headed for Kalaman. He must have known the knights would search for it there. Maybe he plans to hide it in the desert until it's safe to sell somewhere?"

Tumbleweed got stiffly to his feet and walked over to Hector. His tail whipped through the grass behind him like a snake. He sniffed at the tracks Hector pointed out. Then he wrinkled his nose.

"What do you think?" Hector asked.

"I think you smell awful," Tumbleweed said.

Hector groaned, went back to the river, and splashed around until he got all the horse dung off his clothes.

"I think you're right," Tumbleweed said when he came back. "Your invention has a peculiar scent, and I can smell it quite well near the water."

"The acid from the lightning machine. It must have spilled a little as the thief's wagon rolled up the bank. The thief can't be too far ahead. Come on." Hector's spirits lifted a little as he and Tumbleweed followed the tracks out across the grassland.

If he found the thief and the device before the knights, he could try sending a message to Shem again. Maybe, just maybe, things could still work out.

But Hector soon lost the trail in the thick rolling grass.

"Don't worry," Tumbleweed said. "I can still smell it. Might have picked up the scent before if those mountains weren't so full of trees and bushes and little critters. Too many other things to cover the scent. Out here it's just you, me, and the grass. All right, maybe a few bugs, some grass snakes here and there. Oh look, a butterfly. Hello, butterfly. Oh, a hole. I wonder what lives down there." Tumbleweed snuffed at the hole and then called down inside. "You in there. Why don't you come out? I've never smelled anything like you before."

A fuzzy black head with a white stripe poked its nose up and stared at Tumbleweed.

Hector abandoned his friend and bolted away, putting as much space between himself and the skunk as possible.

"Hey, that's not very friendly," Tumbleweed chided Hector. "Just ignore my friend," he said to the skunk.

The skunk lifted its nose disdainfully and vanished back into its hole. Hector breathed a sigh of relief. He could just imagine having to smell Tumbleweed covered in skunk spray all the way back across the desert.

Tumbleweed ambled over to catch up with him. "I think I've lost the thief's trail."

"A skunk will do that to you," Hector said. "Let's keep going in the direction we were before. We're bound to pick it up again as long as you don't get too distracted."

"I wasn't distracted. I was smelling things."

"You were distracted."

"Was not."

"Were too."

"Hey look," Tumbleweed said as they came to the top of a gentle rise and the land sloped down away from them. Far off in the distance, they could see a ribbon of yellow where the grass gave way to the desert. Between them and the desert, a tall, boxy wagon bumped and swayed, pulled by a gray horse.

Chapter Twenty-Seven

Kyani lunged forward, picking up speed. "It's the thief," he roared. He might not be able to fly, but he figured he could run faster than a horse.

"Wait," Hector called. "I can't keep up."

Kyani whirled and scooped Hector up in his claw. "Here. Ride on my back." Kyani lifted Hector up to sit on his shoulders between his wings. "Hold onto my neck frill."

"All right." Hector's tiny hands felt cool against the brassy frill.

Kyani giggled. "Hey, that tickles."

"Sorry," Hector said, but continued to hold on tight.

"Let's go catch a thief." Kyani lowered his head and bolted forward, racing across the grassland. Little by little he gained on the thief.

The thief looked back, saw him, and urged the horse to run faster.

Kyani panted from the exertion of his long run. His

muscles burned. They were used to flying, not racing along the ground.

The horse and wagon disappeared over the edge of the plateau, heading down into the badlands at the desert's edge.

Kyani redoubled his efforts, covering the distance in great bounding strides. He kept his wings folded up tight against his sides so they wouldn't catch the wind. He could smell the desert ahead, hot and dry, inviting him home. Hector's wire stretched overhead, pointing the way.

Hector bounced on Kyani's back with each huge leap forward, but he didn't complain. The gnome's hands on Kyani's neck frill reassured him that his friend hadn't fallen off.

The grass thinned out beneath Kyani's paws, giving way to packed white clay. His claws sank into the ground with each stride. There was the edge. And over. He skidded down the steep incline off the plateau. Gold and red spires towered around him as he bounded down the final slope onto the desert floor.

"Home!" he shouted with delight.

Ahead the horse and wagon careened around a spire and disappeared.

Kyani lowered his head and sped after it. No time to say hello to the rocks and scorpions. He would not let the thief get away. For Hector. The invention was so important to the gnome. Kyani wouldn't let his little friend down.

He skidded around the spire just in time to see the wagon disappear under a sandy arch. If he didn't get closer, he'd lose them in the maze of formations.

Kyani unfurled his wings and flapped hard, lifting himself a foot off the ground, adding momentum to his leaps forward. Pain rippled up from his torn wings, but he ignored it.

Through the arch. Around the side of a cliff. There. The horse and wagon stopped, caught in a wide box canyon on the southeast side of the spires that marked Kyani's lair. The thief turned the wagon around and came face-to-face with Kyani and Hector.

Sheer red cliffs rose high overhead. The wagon had come to a stop beside two spiky rocks protruding from the desert floor. Behind Kyani, Hector's wire stretched across the sand and dived through the bolt-hole into Kyani's lair.

Kyani lowered his wings and stalked to the horse and wagon. The thief stood up on the bench and glared as Kyani approached.

"The thief is just a girl," Hector said in surprise.

It did look like a small female human, but the side of her face was disfigured. She carried no weapon but put her hands on her hips in defiance.

"You stole my friend's invention," Kyani accused. "Give it back now."

"Or what?" the girl said. "Are you going to fry me to a crisp? I'm not scared of you. You're too small to be a real dragon."

Kyani bristled and spread his wings. "I'm a lot bigger than you are."

The thief reached down and grabbed a club from beneath the wagon seat. "Come any closer, and I'll beat you senseless. I hate dragons." From the venom in her voice, Kyani knew she meant it.

He held back, not out of fear, but out of curiosity. "Why?"

"What do you mean, 'Why?'" the girl shouted. "Dragons are evil, cruel, and malicious. They kill every creature around them and burn every building. Come on and attack me. I've been waiting for a chance to avenge my family."

Her words were brave, but her voice wavered.

"She must have been burned by an evil dragon," Hector whispered to Kyani.

Kyani nodded. "Listen," he said, softening his voice. "We don't want to fight you. We just want the invention back. Let us take it, and we'll leave you alone. Maybe we can even help you if you are in some kind of trouble."

"No!" the girl yelled. "You can't help me."

"We could try," Kyani said.

The girl shook her head.

The ground vibrated beneath the wagon.

Kyani looked around in surprise, wondering what would cause the earth to tremble. The girl lost her balance and sat down hard on the bench just as the horse screamed and bolted.

Sand shot up in a geyser where the wagon had been, and with it came a flash of blue.

Kyani gasped as the giant blue dragon burst from the sand. Hector cried out in alarm. The girl and her horse froze, overcome by dragonfear.

The blue dragon settled on top of the sand, its immense body overshadowing Kyani.

"You want to help," the blue dragon said, laughing. "You pitiful little baby."

Its claws shot out and wrapped around Kyani, squeezing him. It happened so fast Kyani didn't have time to dodge. Hector tumbled off him onto the sand, but the blue dragon didn't notice the little gnome.

Kyani trembled with fear as the blue dragon lifted him from the ground. "Run," he yelled to Hector. "Get the girl and go."

The blue dragon shook him. "And to think your parents gave their lives to protect you," he roared. "You. A worthless little lizard who can't even fly."

The Blue tossed Kyani to the ground and sucked in a deep breath. The smell of lightning filled the air.

Kyani scrambled up. "Run!" he yelled at Hector again. Hector blinked and stayed frozen where he stood.

Kyani backed away from the giant blue dragon, away from Hector. "You're a fool," he yelled. "An addled old fool."

The blue dragon opened its jaws and roared, releasing a bolt of blinding white lightning.

CHAPTER TWENTY-EIGHT

Hector's heart beat hard, pounding in his ears. He tried to breathe, but the dragonfear kept him frozen. The giant blue dragon filled the box canyon, wingtip to wingtip. Its vast body glittered like a sapphire in the sand.

Hector heard Tumbleweed yell for him to run, but he was so frightened it seemed like the command was meant for someone else.

Tumbleweed said something to the blue dragon that made it furious. It reared up and let out a bolt of lightning. Tumbleweed dodged to the side, and the lightning melted the sand to glass.

"Stupid, slow, old behemoth!" Tumbleweed shouted. "You'll never catch me."

The blue dragon roared, and the sound shook the sand beneath Hector's feet. His ears rang.

Tumbleweed roared back, a pitiful little yowl compared to the Blue's mighty bellow. Hector dropped to the ground, cowering and covering his ears as the Blue roared again. It lunged at Tumbleweed, but Tumbleweed shot away, out of the canyon into the desert.

The blue dragon lumbered after him, its massive body almost crushing Hector as it passed. A wave of sand, pushed up by its bulk, cast Hector aside at the last moment.

Both dragons moved so fast that Hector caught only a flashing glimpse of bronze and blue as they disappeared around the castlelike spires that marked Tumbleweed's lair.

At last Hector took a breath.

Run! Tumbleweed's command repeated in his head. He realized Tumbleweed had lured the blue dragon away to give Hector a chance to escape. But escape where? He had no chance of outrunning the blue dragon. He looked around, trying to find some safe way out of the badlands.

The horse and wagon still stood close by. The girl cowered on the seat, overcome with dragonfear. Not far away, Hector's wire angled downward and disappeared beneath the sand into Tumbleweed's lair.

"That's it!" Hector shouted, racing to the wagon. He'd never be able to recognize the hidden entrance, but the wire led the way right to it. Of course, that's why the blue dragon had been waiting there. Stringing the wire into the lair had given away its exact position.

Hector cursed himself as he reached the wagon and climbed up onto the seat. He took the reins and slapped them against the horse's back. "Yah."

The horse laid his ears back and rolled his eyes but didn't move.

"Oh come on," Hector said. "We have to get out of here."

He tried slapping the reins again, but the horse remained rooted in place. The cliffs and spires echoed with the dragons' roars.

Hector shook the girl. "Snap out of it. Come on."

She blinked, and her eyes focused on Hector. "The fire," she cried. "The fire. I have to get them out." She jumped to her feet, but Hector pulled her back down and handed her the reins.

"Follow the wire," he ordered. "Straight into the sand."

The ground shook, and the blue dragon lumbered back into view, snarling in fury. The girl gripped the reins and nodded to the horse.

The gray whinnied and broke into a sudden gallop. The poles that held the wire flashed past them. The blue dragon roared, leaped into the air, and dived at them.

The last pole disappeared behind the wagon, and the horse vanished into the sand. Then the wagon slipped through, Hector and the girl with it. Sand showered over them—suffocating, thick—and then gave way. The horse's hooves thudded against the tunnel floor.

Hector gasped and wiped the gritty sand from his face. Behind them the blue dragon roared and flung himself at the entrance. Only his nose fit through. The sight of the dragon's snapping jaws terrified the horse and it bolted forward, carrying them deeper into Tumbleweed's lair.

Darkness fell around them, and the horse stopped, quivering.

"I think the tunnel has ended," the girl whispered.

"No. It splits in two directions here. Turn to the left."

"How do you know?" The girl hesitated. Behind them the blue dragon continued to roar and tear at the tunnel entrance.

"Just trust me." Hector sat rigid in his seat. He didn't know how long it would take the blue dragon to tunnel in after them. Not long enough, he was sure. The girl urged the horse onward in the dark, turning to the left. "Do you think he killed the little dragon?"

Hector had been trying not to think about it at all. His eyes stung. "Tumbleweed!" he called. His voice echoed along the tunnel. "Tumbleweed." His own voice bounced back to him and was lost in the blue dragon's roars.

They came to another intersection. "Turn left," Hector directed.

The girl gave the horse the command, and it continued forward in the dark. A warm yellow glow flickered to life ahead. They came out in the foyer above the steps of the Grand Conversation Hall. A fire danced in the massive fireplace, lighting the crystals on the roof.

The girl gasped. "So beautiful."

"Yes, beautiful," Hector said, but his eyes were fixed on the brass dragon quivering in front of the fire. He jumped from the wagon and raced down the steps. "Tumbleweed, are you all right?"

"Hector!" Tumbleweed leaped up and danced in a circle. "You're alive. You escaped." He scooped Hector up and licked his face with his rough tongue.

Hector laughed and hugged the edge of Tumbleweed's skull plate. "Are you hurt?"

Tumbleweed shook his head. "My tail end is a bit singed, and my sore wings are killing me, but I'm all right. Just scared. I didn't think you'd made it inside in time. But here you are." He licked Hector again and then gazed up at the girl, her horse, and her wagon. "I think some introductions are in order. My name is Tumbleweed, and this is Hector. Who are you, and why did you take the invention?"

The girl tore her gaze away from the crystals in the ceiling and climbed from the wagon. She came down the steps slowly, running her fingers over the gilded edges and smooth marble. "This place is richer than a king's palace."

Hector folded his arms and glared at her. "Tumbleweed asked you your name. I suggest you tell us."

The girl looked up at Hector and Tumbleweed as if surprised to see them there. "My name. Yes." Her eyes fell on the exquisite statues flanking the fireplace. Her mouth dropped open and no more words came out.

"You like my home?" Tumbleweed asked, swelling with pride. "It is beautiful, isn't it? The best place in all the world. This is the Grand Conversation Hall. We come here to talk."

"Right. Talk," Hector said icily. "As in, tell us your name."

The girl walked past Hector and reached up to stroke the closest dragon statue. "Dani."

"What?" Hector said.

"My name's Dani, and I stole your invention because a blue dragon burned my house and killed my family. I have nothing left. I don't even look human anymore."

She covered her scarred face with her hand. "I need steel to survive, so I took it."

Tumbleweed let out a sympathetic rumble. "My parents are dead too. Killed by that blue monster outside. I've been lonely here until Hector came along. Do you ever get lonely?"

Dani nodded. "All the time. No one wants to talk to me. I look so ugly."

Tumbleweed lifted his claw and gently rubbed the side of her scarred face. "I don't think you look that bad. In fact, I think you're quite beautiful."

Pain lanced through Hector's heart. He remembered Amber's cool hands against his bald head. She'd said something similar. She cared about him more than anyone. He should never have yelled at her or argued with her. Somehow he had to get back and make things right.

A blistering roar filled the hall from close by in the tunnel. Too close. The ground shook. One of the giant crystals broke loose and crashed to the floor, just missing Hector.

"You can't hide from me," the blue dragon bellowed. "I'll tear this whole lair apart to get to you."

Chapter Twenty-nine

Hector jumped. The blue dragon had torn through the ground even faster than he'd feared. The sandstone crumbled too easily beneath its massive claws. But they were deeper than the sandstone here in the Grand Conversation Hall, down in harder rock. The chamber shivered against the blue dragon's onslaught.

"It's not safe!" Hector cried. "Get back in the wagon. We've got to get out the other side before this whole cave collapses in on us." Hector grabbed Dani's hand and dragged her back up to her wagon.

"But there's nowhere to hide out there," Tumbleweed protested.

Another giant crystal broke free and crashed to the marble floor, splintering into a shower of shards. Tumble-weed yelped and raced up the stairs after Hector. "This way," Tumbleweed called and guided the horse into a tunnel that branched off from the foyer.

Darkness fell around them as they moved away from

the fire. Soon, Hector could see nothing, not even his hand in front of his face.

Dani sat on the bench beside him, her muscles tense. Hector could hear the shuffle of Tumbleweed's body ahead and the horse's hooves plopping on the sand. He couldn't see, but he felt the walls closing in around him.

The top of the house on the back of the wagon caught against something above and held for a second. Then the corner splintered and the wagon jolted forward. The soft, sandy floor gave way to harder rock, and the horse's steps became more pronounced pings.

Hector had never been in this part of the cave before. It continued on and on, dark and dreadful. But the blue dragon's roars faded in the distance.

The wagon stopped. "Hold on a minute," Tumbleweed said. He grunted, and a loud scraping sound filled the passage. "Hidden door. Had to move the rock. We should be able to get through now. We'll come out a false entry on the north side, not far from where your wire emerges and heads off to Kaal."

"Maybe we should stay down here for a while," Dani said. "Tumbleweed's right. Up there we're easy game for the dragon."

Hector gritted his teeth and rubbed his head, trying to think. If they could get away while the blue dragon was still digging on the other side of the spires, they'd have a chance to survive. If they waited, the blue dragon might get bored and start looking for other ways in, or it'd succeed in collapsing the whole mountain on top of their heads. They could still hear the dim echo of the dragon's roaring and scraping behind them.

A deep rumble filled the hall, and the ground shook. The cart swayed. The rocks above them groaned. "Go forward!" Hector screamed. "Get us out of here. We have to head for Kaal. It's our only chance."

Dani urged the horse into a gallop. The wagon lurched forward. The ceiling crashed down behind them, burying the tunnel they'd taken from the Grand Conversation Hall.

A dim light appeared ahead, and Tumbleweed stopped them in the mouth of a cave. A wide, easy slope led down to the desert floor below.

Tumbleweed stood panting beside the cart, scanning the sky and ground. Hector joined him in the search for the blue dragon. He saw nothing but cacti, sagebrush, and sand—and his poles with the wire stretching out in a straight line to meet the horizon.

"It's got to still be behind us," Hector said. "How else would it have caused the cave-in?"

"Right. Let me go first." Tumbleweed took a shaky step out into the sunlight. Nothing happened. "I guess it's safe. I don't see it anywhere." He motioned for the others to come out.

Dani signaled the horse and it started forward, breaking into a smooth lope. Hector glanced up, side to side, and back over his shoulder at the red spires. His heart raced. Dragonfear paralyzed him, but there was no sign of the dragon.

Tumbleweed loped along beside them down the slope. Dani steered the horse over to run next to the wires. No chance of getting lost. They just needed to drive hard and fast to Kaal. Hector shook his head. It would be a miracle if they made it. Too bad Sir Guyon and his knights weren't around now.

Tumbleweed slowed, sniffing the air. "Something's wrong," he said.

"What do you mean?" Hector twisted every which way, looking for the blue dragon but not seeing it or anything else threatening.

"The desert smells wrong."

A hot wind whipped a cloud of sand up around the cart. It stung Hector's face, and he lifted his arm to shield it. Then the wind died down as suddenly as it had come.

Tumbleweed whirled around. "No birds in the cacti. No bugs. No snakes. No scorpions. Nothing. I've never seen the desert like this."

The horse whinnied as if in fearful agreement.

"Just keep going," Hector said. "We have to get away before the blue dragon figures out we've left the lair."

A shimmer flashed around the spires, and the blue dragon appeared and dived at them.

"Turn around!" Tumbleweed screamed. "We have to get back in the cave!"

As if in answer, the blue dragon settled its massive body onto the sand, blocking their way back. He towered high above Hector's wire and filled the air with its deep, booming laughter.

"I knew I could flush you out. Did you think you could outrun me?" It clawed the horse aside.

Tumbleweed jumped in between the blue dragon and the wagon, spreading his wings and snarling. "It's me you want. Leave these other creatures alone. They're nothing to you."

The blue dragon laughed again. "So brave. So willing to die, just like your parents."

Hector shuddered. Tumbleweed would die for him while he sat there on the bench frozen with fear.

No. Anger burned through him. He plunged his hands in his apron pocket searching for some weapon, something he could use against the dragon. Screwdriver, wrench . . . His hands closed on the pair of wire cutters.

"Just let them go." Tumbleweed's voice shook.

"Maybe, just for sport, I'll let them go while I finish you off. Then I'll catch them. That will make the hunt more fun. What do you think they'll do, go back to the cave or head off across the desert?"

"Neither!" Hector shouted. He scrambled up on top of the roof of the little wagon house and spread his arms to where his fingers almost touched the wire he'd hung across the desert from pole to pole. "We won't run. We'll stand and fight. I won't let you kill my friend."

The blue dragon snorted. "You? You're not even half the size of one of my scales." He reached out and grabbed Tumbleweed by the tail, lifting him in the air above Hector's head.

Tumbleweed roared in fright and let out a flaming breath against the blue dragon's leg.

The blue dragon laughed. "Care to try your sleep gas next?" It bent down, putting its giant head close to Tumbleweed's small face. Its eyes glittered deadly blue, so close Hector could have touched them if he ran forward to the edge of the roof. But he stayed back and held his breath while Tumbleweed let out a puff of sleeping gas.

The blue dragon huffed, and the gas curled away from its face.

"Now it's my turn," the Blue said, sucking in a breath. Lightning crackled between its teeth.

Hector's skin prickled. So close. Where he stood on the wagon, the lightning would shoot right over him into Tumbleweed.

Tumbleweed squirmed and flapped in the blue dragon's clutches.

Chapter Thirty

Hector tensed, waiting for the blue dragon's huge blast of burning death.

The dragon let the lightning build and build, holding it in, its eyes sparkling in cruel glee at Tumbleweed's pitiful roars and struggles to get free.

Hector's hand shook, but he clutched the wire cutter in a steely grip. The scent of ozone filled the air, and the lightning writhed around the dragon's jaws until the Blue could hold it in no longer.

The blue dragon breathed out, releasing a thunderous bolt of lightning.

Hector threw himself against the copper wire, bending it back with all his weight, and then severed it with the wire cutters.

The wire snapped forward, just missing Tumbleweed, passing in front of him into the oncoming bolt of lightning.

The wire caught the lightning and continued its arc, snapping dead center across the blue dragon's face. The full blast of the ancient dragon's destructive power channeled into its molten blue eyes.

The blue dragon bellowed in agony, dropped Tumbleweed, and clawed at its eyes.

Hector's weight against the severed wire propelled him off the side of the wagon. He fell with a thump into the sand. He could see under the wagon to where Tumbleweed lay limp and unmoving while the blue dragon thrashed in pain and anger, its wings kicking up a pounding spray of dirt, and its legs and torso thundering against the ground.

Hector raced underneath the wagon to the other side where Tumbleweed lay. "Tumbleweed, get up! You'll be trampled."

The blue dragon's enraged roar shook the ground and made Hector's ears ring. The dragon's tail snapped around and hit the wagon house, splintering the walls to slivers that rained down on Hector and Tumbleweed.

The crash of wood against Tumbleweed's head roused him to action. He rose to his feet and lunged aside to keep from being whipped by the blue dragon's thrashing tail. "It's blind," Tumbleweed said, gazing up at his tormentor.

"Right, and it'll still kill us if we don't get out of its way," Hector warned.

Tumbleweed grabbed Hector in one claw and Dani from the wagon bench with his other claw and raced away.

Hector wrapped his arms around Tumbleweed's claw and urged the little dragon on. Behind them the blue dragon tore apart the ground and filled the sky with angry lightning until the fire in its belly gave out. Uttering a long, mournful bellow, it flapped its giant wings and took to the air. Flying blind, it careened into one of the rocky spires, knocking the tip off. Changing course, the dragon winged eastward over the sand dunes, disappearing into a wall of billowing brown air.

Tumbleweed stopped and dropped to the ground, gasping for air. He opened his claws, releasing Hector and Dani.

Dani scrambled away, walked a few yards, then sat on the sand and wept. Hector felt like doing the same, but he had to be sure Tumbleweed was all right.

"Tumbleweed," he said, "are you hurt?" He ran his fingers along Tumbleweed's scaly leg. Tumbleweed didn't respond, just kept his gaze fixed on the eastern sky where the blue dragon had vanished.

"Tumbleweed?" Hector tried to shake the dragon, a useless gesture because of his size.

Tumbleweed tore his eyes away from the horizon and looked down. "Hector, you . . . your device . . . the knights were right. It is a weapon. You just blinded a blue dragon with its own lightning. No one will believe it. A single gnome defeats an ancient blue dragon." He shook his head in amazement, then licked Hector's face. "You're the best, Hector. You really are."

Hector wiped his face with his shirt sleeve. "So are you, Tumbleweed. That took a lot of courage to throw yourself in front of the blue dragon to save us. If you'd run, you could have gotten away and hidden in the sand."

"You're my friend. I'd never desert you like that." He patted Hector's back a bit too enthusiastically, knocking him to the sand.

Hector laughed. "If you're all right, I think I better go see to Dani."

"I'm fine," Tumbleweed said, then lifted his gaze back to the brown skyline.

Hector walked over to Dani and sat in the sand next to her. Her sobs broke the desert silence. Her eyes were red and puffy, and she rocked back and forth in misery.

"Are you hurt?" Hector asked, putting a comforting arm around her shoulders.

"No. I'm just a wretched, awful person," she wailed.

"You're not so bad," Hector said. "Tumbleweed and I already told you we don't mind your looks. Don't worry. Everything is going to be all right now."

"No. No. It will never be all right. You and Tumbleweed are so brave and good, and I'm a complete idiot. And now I've lost Felicity. I have nothing left."

Hector pulled a sand-covered handkerchief with a few grease stains from his apron and handed it to her. "I was just as afraid of the dragon as you were. You can't be ashamed of dragonfear. It does that to everyone."

Dani took the handkerchief and dabbed at her tear-streaked face. "No. It's not that. Don't you get it? I'm a thief. I think only of myself. I take other people's things. I told myself I had to because my parents are dead and I needed to survive, but it's still not right. I've been selfish, and I've hurt people, even someone who trusted me and was nice to me. And I stole your invention. I ruined everything for you. Just everything."

She fell into a fit of hacking sobs that surprised Hector with its intensity.

"I don't know," Hector said. "I think the knights and dwarves were doing a good job of ruining everything before you ever arrived. Everyone wants to use my invention as a weapon, but I never intended it for that."

He shoved his hand in his apron pocket, pulled out the wire cutters, and twisted them in his fingers. "Even I used my invention as a weapon. I had to. The dragon would have killed us all. I seem to be good at making weapons and terrible at communication."

"You're not so bad." Dani took his hand and squeezed it. "You're doing a great job talking to me. Thank you." She sniffed and wiped her eyes.

Hector coughed and looked out across the desert toward Kaal. "I should have listened to Amber all those times she tried to talk to me. I never told her how I felt about her, and she's my best friend in the whole world."

That sent Dani into a fresh bout of tears.

"Come on. It's all right," Hector said. "I'm going to go back to Kaal, find Amber, and have a good long talk with her. I'll do whatever it takes to work things out."

Dani stopped crying and looked up, taking small, hiccuping breaths. "That's it. I'll do the same. I'll go with you and apologize to Amber, and then I'll return all the fabric that I stole from the Goodlunds."

"You stole fabric from the Goodlunds!" Hector said, jumping up. "But they're my friends."

Dani nodded. "I know. I've been so dumb. But I can make it right. I don't expect you or them to forgive me, but I will return everything I've stolen." Her face fell, and a single remaining tear slipped from her eyes. "I don't know how I'll survive though. I have nothing left. No family. No land. Not even Felicity."

A soft whinny interrupted her. "I think this belongs to you," Tumbleweed said from behind them. He nudged Dani's gray horse with his snout.

"Felicity," Dani said, jumping up to hug the horse's neck.

"I think his leg is hurt," Tumbleweed said. "I found him limping around, looking for you."

"At least he's alive," Dani said, checking Felicity over. "I thought that horrible dragon had killed him. He doesn't look too bad. He should recover."

A deep rumbling growl rose in the distance. Tumbleweed twitched and looked at the darkening eastern skyline. "I think we should go back to my lair."

"What is it? What's wrong? Is the blue dragon coming back?" Hector could see Tumbleweed shaking.

"No," Tumbleweed said. "Something far worse than a blue dragon."

The roar grew louder until it became deafening. Hector realized the wall of billowing brown had grown taller and was racing straight at them.

"What is it?" he asked, a rock forming in his stomach. The air sucked away from around them. He had a good idea what it was, but didn't want to believe it.

"A sandstorm," Tumbleweed said in awe. "The biggest one I've ever seen. No wonder all the desert animals are hiding. We need to get inside. That thing will kill everything in its path."

CHAPTER THIRTY-ONE

Hector looked back to the broken rock formation that housed Tumbleweed's lair. If they hurried, they might make it back before the sandstorm reached them.

"Come on. Let's go," Hector yelled, his voice barely audible above the storm's growl. He raced back for the lair, hoping the blue dragon hadn't demolished all of it.

"Wait," Dani said. "We can't leave the wagon. It's got your invention and the material I have to take back to the Goodlunds."

Hector stopped. A horrible thought rumbled in his mind with the storm: Tumbleweed said that it would kill everything in its path. He thought about Kaal's walls. They could keep out any enemy except the Bronze Giant or a sandstorm.

"Amber!" Hector yelled, racing to the wagon. "I've got to warn her." He leaped up into the back of the wagon. The blue dragon had broken the boxy house, leaving the insides open to the sky. He found his sender-receiver device shoved up against the little cookstove. "Tumble-weed, help me lift this over to the wire. I've got to attach it to the line."

"Hector, there's no time. We have to get inside." Tumbleweed tried to grab Hector, but Hector ducked under his claw and rolled the device off the back of the wagon. It bumped to the ground with a loud crash but remained intact.

"Tumbleweed, get Dani and the horse and wagon inside," Hector ordered. "I'll follow, I promise." He raced over to where the wire to Kaal was hanging.

Dani had the horse hooked to the wagon and urged Felicity to hurry toward the lair, but he couldn't manage more than a slow, painful walk. The leg injury coupled with pulling the wagon through the soft sand was too much.

Tumbleweed roared in frustration, picked up Felicity, tucked him under his foreleg, and ran for the lair, pulling Dani and the wagon behind him.

"Good boy," Hector whispered. He got out his tools and spliced the end of the wire into his sender-receiver device. Sand whipped up around him, stinging his eyes, making it hard to see. The coming wall of brown blocked out the sun. Its roar shook the ground.

Hector pulled the lever, powering up the machine. He got his finger on the sender arm and tapped out a message.

Amber,

Huge sandstorm coming. Get everyone inside. Stay safe.

Love,

Hector

A sudden blast of wind knocked him to the ground and sent his invention tumbling away, snapping the wire. Sand tore at Hector's clothes, shredding them. Unable to stand, he crawled toward the lair, praying he'd sent the message in time, and that Amber had gotten it.

In less than a minute, the sand tore away his clothes and clawed his skin. It filled his mouth and eyes and ears. He couldn't breathe. I'm drowning in sand, he thought. He'd survived the sandstorm that had broken his flying machine and carried him out into the desert, but that one had been small compared to the monster that consumed him now.

His arms and legs gave out, and he fell to the ground. At least Amber will be safe, he thought.

Amber crept along the crowded streets. It was market day in Kaal, and everyone seemed to be out, buying and selling, thronging the streets, filling the air with cheerful voices.

Normally Amber liked cheerful people and happy sounds. They made life worthwhile even when things looked the very worst. But today she resented them. They made it so much harder for her to get out of the jail and to the lab without getting caught.

The guards had been alert, and she'd barely made it outside without being seen. She wondered if they were catching on to her frequent absences from the jail, but she couldn't just sit around in a cell when word might come from Hector anytime. At least she hoped it would.

Two days had passed since she'd sent her warning, and he'd never responded. All the horrible things that could have happened to him filled her thoughts as she darted across the street, using a cart to conceal her as she made her way to the lab's secret back entrance.

She pushed a button that looked like a knot of wood in the back wall. A slot opened up, and she peeked through the crack to get a view of the lab beyond. The workbench lay in shadow. The light from the front window had turned to a muted gray. The lab sat silent and empty.

Amber stepped out and crept over to the sender-receiver at the back of the room. The receiver arm rested immobile in its place. Everything was the same as she'd left it on her last visit from prison. Except, wait. The paper had scrolled forward.

With a cry of excitement Amber tore it off and lifted it to see the dots and lines in the dim light. The front door rattled. Amber jumped, then realized it was only a strong gust of wind and not the guards.

With shaking hands she opened the code book and flipped through the pages.

AMBER.

Right. Amber, of course. Now what?

HUGE.

Huge what? Frantically Amber turned back and forth through the book looking up the next letters.

SANDSTORM.

Sandstorm? She raced to the window. The sky overhead was blue, but an uneasy feeling gripped her. She returned to the message. It didn't take her long to decipher the rest.

When she finished, she stood with the paper shaking in her hands. She had to tell Shem. She had to warn the city. If the storm hit while everyone was outside, hundreds of people could be hurt or killed.

But if she took the message to Shem, he wouldn't believe her.

Still shaking, she let herself out the back door to the street outside. Tucking the message in her apron, she raced to the bell tower, not caring if anyone saw her, just running as fast as she could.

She reached the base of the tower and started up the long flight of steps to the top. Around and around she went, climbing higher and higher. Breathless, she lunged up the last few steps and raced to the railing. The tower was the highest point in the city. The great warning bell waited in silence.

Amber gazed out across the eastern horizon. A dark wall of sand swept toward her, moving so fast it would reach Kaal in only a few minutes.

No time. Amber sprang to the bell rope and pulled with all her might. Her small size moved the bell, but not far enough to bring it against the clapper.

She jumped up, catching the rope above her head and using all her weight to pull it down.

The bell swung again. A single soft bong sounded.

She jumped again, pulling the rope harder. Jump, pull. Jump, pull. The bell swung in wider and wider arcs. The clapper bonged against the side, softly at first and then louder and louder, a warning call. Danger! Danger!

People looked up. A brown haze covered the sun, and the air sucked away.

"Sandstorm!" someone cried.

People shouted in alarm and rushed for the buildings. A thunderous growl filled the air and rattled the tower.

The wall of sand slammed into the city and reached out for Amber. She loosened her grip on the bell rope and slid down it into the tower.

A screaming whoosh of sand followed her. As soon as her feet touched the bottom, she dived under the stairs, curled into a ball, and covered her face with her hands.

CHAPTER THIRTY~TWO

Kyani crawled out of the tunnel into the blinding, howling sand. It scraped across his scales and stung his eyes. He could see nothing. Squeezing his eyes closed to protect them, he inched forward, sniffing for Hector's scent. He tried to picture in his mind the exact spot where he'd left his friend, desperately sending a message on his machine. Kyani had taken Dani, the horse, and the wagon deep inside a section of his lair that had not collapsed.

"Hector," he called, but the wind swallowed his voice so he couldn't even hear himself.

The sand pounded against him, trying to knock him over and send him tumbling away. He dropped flat on the ground and pulled himself forward with his claws. The scent of blood came to him amidst the fury of the storm, and he turned toward it.

Bit by bit, claw by claw, he dragged himself forward until his nose came in contact with a blood-covered lump in the sand.

Hector. The sand had torn away his clothing and cut his skin. Only his leather apron remained. Kyani curled his body around the gnome and spread his wing over the top of him, creating a protective shelter. The wind caught at his wing, trying to tear it up and off, but Kyani burrowed the edge down into the sand and tucked his head beneath it next to Hector.

"Hector, are you alive?" he whispered.

The little body stirred, and Hector reached up and touched Kyani's wing. He ran his fingers down the membrane and over the scales of his torso.

Kyani giggled at his feathery touch.

Hector coughed the sand out of his lungs. "Yes, I'm alive. Why aren't you in the lair?"

Kyani licked the blood from Hector's head and face. "You think I'd leave you out here alone?"

"You should have stayed inside. Now we'll both be killed." Hector's voice was warm and friendly, though his words stung.

"Don't worry," Kyani said. "The wind and sand won't hurt my scales. As long as I keep my wings tucked close and my head beneath them, I'll be all right. It's you I'm worried about. You look awful."

"I'm doing better now that I can breathe." Hector inched closer to Kyani's side. "How long do you think the storm will last?"

"I don't know. But I bet we have plenty of time for a long talk."

Hector laughed. "I'm sure we do."

Hector stirred. He wasn't sure when he'd drifted off, somewhere in the middle of Tumbleweed's long oration. The first thing Hector noticed was the ringing silence. He opened his eyes and found himself in a pitch black cocoon beneath Tumbleweed's wing. The air tasted stale and did little to alleviate his sudden feeling of suffocation.

"Tumbleweed," he said, reaching out and tapping the dragon's skull plate. Tumbleweed, too, had fallen asleep while they waited out the storm.

Tumbleweed yawned and licked Hector's face. "You all right?" he asked.

"No," Hector said. "I can't breathe. I think we're running out of air.

"Oh." Tumbleweed grunted, trying to lift his wing, but it refused to move. "I think we're buried."

Hector gasped and tried to squash the rising feeling of panic that threatened to overcome him.

"Don't worry," Tumbleweed said. "I can dig us out. Brass dragons are great at burrowing. "Close your eyes and take a deep breath."

Hector did as he was told and felt a shower of sand fall around him, burying him from head to toe. Then Tumbleweed's claw pushed through the sand and grabbed him, jerking him upward.

Sand tore at his lacerated skin. His lungs screamed for air, but he kept his lips clenched tight as Tumbleweed dragged him up and up. At last they burst out of the sand into the desert sunlight.

Hector brushed the sand off his face and gasped, filling his lungs with air.

"Good morning," Tumbleweed said, spreading his wings to catch the sun's rays. "Looks like the storm lasted the night. Wow, look at the desert."

Hector stared out across a flat golden expanse. All life had vanished—cacti, Tumbleweed, and sagebrush—all buried beneath the endless sand. He strained to see any sign of his sender-receiver device or the poles and wires he'd worked so hard to set up.

There was nothing. It had all vanished as if nothing had ever been there.

Hector swallowed and turned back to the red spires that marked Tumbleweed's lair. The tops had been sheared off by the force of the storm, and they stood no more than a cluster of cones sticking up from the sand.

"Where's Dani?" he asked, shaken.

"I left her inside." Tumbleweed followed Hector's

gaze, looking back to the lair.

"The entrance is buried," Hector said. "Even more buried than usual. Do you think you can get in?"

"Sure. It's just a matter of digging another tunnel."

"How long will that take?" Hector asked, rubbing his head. "Ouch." The wind had torn off a layer of skin, and his head hurt at the touch, but he'd been lucky. Tumbleweed had found him before the storm had stripped all the meat off his bones. He shoved his hands in his apron pockets, glad that it at least had survived the storm.

"It might take a while. But there's a secret passage up on top between the spires that we should be able to get to. Come on."

Kyani led Hector back to the shortened spires.

Hector followed, forcing his reluctant body to move. The thought of the cool pool of water in the sleep chamber carried him forward.

Tumbleweed paused beside the base of the spire, broken by the blue dragon. He ran his claw along the red rock and then pushed in. The rock gave way, opening a smooth tunnel beyond. Tumbleweed whooped with delight and pranced inside. Hector had to duck to keep from getting hit by Tumbleweed's tail in his excitement.

"Dani," Tumbleweed called as he danced down the tunnel. "Dani! We're here. We're all right."

A strange silence answered them.

CHAPTER THIRTY-THREE

Hector followed Tumbleweed through the tunnel down into the main part of the lair. They came out through a hidden door into the foyer above the Grand Conversation Hall. The steps were littered with shattered crystal, and a pile of boulders and rubble near the back showed where the blue dragon had tried to claw his way in.

"Not too bad," Tumbleweed said, picking his way down the stairs. "It could have been worse. The statues are fine. We can clean this mess up in no time."

Hector took a deep breath. Yes, the chamber could be repaired. He was glad for Tumbleweed. "Where did you leave Dani?"

"In the tunnel on the far side of the Hall of Art." Tumbleweed waved to the opening that led out the opposite side of the Grand Conversation Hall.

"That's the hall where you keep your treasure?"

"Yes. Sure. If you want to call it that. I think 'art' sounds better, don't you?"

Without answering, Hector bolted across the vast hall, dodging fallen crystals and scrambling up the far steps. He passed under the high arch into the treasure hall.

Dani stood fingering the great tapestry. In her other hand she held the vase decorated with steel coins.

"Dani," Hector said, lifting his hand and taking a step forward, glad he had his apron to cover his front side.

Dani jumped and hid the vase behind her back. "Oh, Hector. I didn't hear you come in."

Hector folded his arms across his chest and tapped his foot. "I thought you'd given up stealing."

Dani's face turned red. "I-I wasn't stealing," she stammered, fumbling to put the vase back. "I was just admiring all the beautiful things. Look at this." She ran her hand along the twisted piece of wood that graced the center of the room. "Do you know what this is?"

"A dead tree?"

Dani gave a short bark of laughter. "This is a piece of vallenwood from Solace."

"So?"

Dani rolled her eyes. "Look at these fabrics." She pointed to the row of shimmering materials draped along one side. "These make the fabric I stole from the Goodlunds look like rags. I never dreamed things like this could exist."

"You like my Hall of Art?" Tumbleweed asked, trotting

in. "Beautiful, isn't it? Of course I didn't collect all this stuff. My parents did."

"It's glorious," Dani said, her eyes shining with delight. "This whole lair is more beautiful than any place I've ever dreamed of. What is this? Where did it come from?" She lifted the vase she'd been holding when Hector dashed in.

"Oh, that." Tumbleweed pranced over to her and launched into a long-winded description of one of his father's earliest treasure-hunting expeditions. Dani listened, mesmerized by Tumbleweed's story.

Hector left the two happily conversing and made his way to the sleep chamber. He drank the cool water from the pool. Then he took off his apron and slipped into the comforting water to wash the blood and sand from his body.

Tumbleweed walked in about the time he finished his bath. "Hey, Hector. Dani said you might need this." He held up a shiny green suit with a gold collar and cuffs. "She went through all my chests of clothing to find something that might fit."

"Thank you," Hector said, taking the outfit. He didn't bother asking why a dragon would have chests of clothing. Tumbleweed's parents seemed to collect everything.

Tumbleweed stretched out on the giant rock bed and dangled his front legs over the side, swinging them back and forth. "I like Dani," he said. "I've asked her to stay here with me."

Hector pulled the shirt over his head and turned down the collar. "What did she say?"

"Yes, of course. Who wouldn't want to live here?" He eyed Hector. "Oh, let me see. You. Crazy gnome. And now your talking machine is gone, destroyed by the sandstorm. Sorry about that. But when you go, I'll be all alone here, and Dani's alone, an orphan just like me, and she wants to stay here so neither of us ever has to be lonely again."

"That's wonderful." Relief swept through Hector. He'd wondered how he would talk Tumbleweed into letting him leave now that his sender-receiver device had been buried by the sandstorm.

Tumbleweed leaned forward and licked Hector's face. "I know you want to go home. When my wings are better, I'll fly you to Kaal, but I'll miss you when you're gone."

"I'll miss you too," Hector said, rubbing Tumbleweed's skull plate. "But don't worry. I've got a bunch of new ideas about how to send messages back and forth. I'll stay in touch. I promise."

"There it is," Hector said as Tumbleweed flew him toward Kaal. It had taken several weeks for Tumbleweed's wings to heal enough to take Hector and the Goodlund's fabric to the city.

"Wow," Tumbleweed said. "Look at those walls. Look at those buildings. Is that the Bronze Giant you told me about? I'd love to add him to my parents' collection, though I don't think he'd fit in the lair. Can you believe that? He's buried in sand up to his thighs. Must have been the storm. I hope the people in the city are all right."

"Me too," Hector said.

Tumbleweed folded his wings to land in front of the gate, but Hector urged him to fly straight over the wall. People looked up from their laborious work of digging out the sand from the city streets and gasped as Tumbleweed flew past.

"This way." Hector pointed out the lab, and Tumbleweed settled onto the road outside.

A pair of city guards flanked the doorway. They drew their swords and tried to appear brave in the face of the unexpected dragon.

"Hector," one of the guards said. "You're not allowed in this city. I think you better take your dragon and leave."

"What? Shem didn't get my message?" Hector asked, his heart racing. Tumbleweed let Hector down onto the road. He ran up to the door, but the guard grabbed him before he could go in.

"Sorry, no one gets in here." The guard lifted him off the ground. "I'll have to take you to the prison and send word to Shem."

Tumbleweed roared and stabbed a claw against the guard's chest. "Put my friend down."

The guard dropped Hector and backed against the building, shaking.

"Where's Amber?" Hector demanded. "I know she's here. She sent me a message from my sender-receiver, and I sent one back to her warning her about the sandstorm."

"Impossible," the guard said. "She's been locked in prison."

"What?" Hector shouted, clenching his fists. "She's done nothing wrong."

"I had no choice," said a voice from behind.

Hector whipped around to see Shem walk up along with Peyote and a dozen of his men.

"She refused to tell me how to dismantle your invention." Shem shrugged as if the entire matter were out of his hands.

"And a good thing she did too," Hector said. "If she'd dismantled it, how would you have gotten warning of the sandstorm in time? I flew over the city. Everyone seems to be all right, so she must have given you the message."

Shem shook his head. "I don't know what you're talking about."

Peyote cleared his throat. "We did find Amber in the bell tower after the sandstorm. She had these on her." He pulled out a strip of paper and Hector's code book. "Just looked like scribbles to me. Didn't seem important."

Shem took the paper and code book. He twisted the paper this way and that, squinting at what appeared to be random marks.

"It's the message from the sender-receiver device," Hector said, taking care to pronounce his sentence and not run his words together. "The series of dots and lines stand for letters. The code book there tells you what they mean."

Shem opened the code book, stared at it for a moment, and then snapped it shut.

"You see? My invention worked. It saved your city." Hector held his breath, trying to stay calm. Shem would have to understand now.

"Thank you, Hector." Shem reached down and handed Hector the message and book. "I guess I never understood what you were trying to do." He frowned and looked up at the lab. "But you need to understand, what you've created is dangerous. I know you intend to use it for good, and you have. But innocent people could get hurt around it, and some people might do terrible things with it if they get their hands on it. I'd hate to see that happen."

Hector hung his head and kicked at the sand. He knew how dangerous lightning could be. He'd faced a blue dragon after all. Though he'd turned the lightning back on the Blue, Hector knew he never wanted to deal with something like that again.

"You want me to dismantle my device?" The sender-receiver in the lab was all that remained of his hard work, the last tiny part of the invention he had thought would fulfill his Life Quest. But he'd been wrong. It hadn't fulfilled his quest. It had only started him on the right path.

"Yes. I want it taken apart safely," Shem said.

Hector nodded. "And if I do it, you'll let Amber out of prison?"

"Yes, of course. And you'll both be welcome here in Kaal for as long as you like, provided you don't rebuild that invention." Shem put a fatherly hand on Hector's shoulder. "It's for the best."

Tumbleweed cleared his throat and growled. "Hector doesn't have to do anything he doesn't want to. You'll let him leave with his device and Amber, or I'll see to it that he does."

The guards stiffened and reached for their weapons.

"No. It's all right, Tumbleweed," Hector said, patting his big friend. "I think Shem's right. The world isn't ready for this invention yet. But I have plenty of other inventions to keep me busy. This is just the beginning."

He walked past the guards, pushed open the door, and stepped into the lab. The worktable sat empty, and the heady smells of grease, melted wax, and acid that had filled it were gone. Only the smell of Amber's favorite soap lingered on the air. She had been there. She had gotten his message and warned the town. Poor Amber was locked up in prison because she'd refused to take apart his invention.

Hector shook his head, pulled out his screwdriver, and went over to the sender-receiver device.

CHAPTER THIRTY-FOUR

Hector stacked the last piece of the sender-receiver on the workbench amid all the wire, flasks of acid, bits of copper and zinc, and other scattered parts of what once had been his grand invention.

The lab door squeaked open, and he looked up, thinking he needed to oil its hinges.

Amber stood in the doorway. Her clothes were rumpled and her tawny hair a tangled mess.

"Amber," he said, dropping his tools and jumping to his feet. "You're the most beautiful person I've ever set eyes on." He scrambled over the worktable, down the other side, and met her halfway across the room, wrapping her in his arms. The tools in their aprons clanked together as they embraced.

"Amber, I'm so sorry," he said, running his fingers through her thick hair.

"I am too," Amber said.

"I never should have left you," they both said at the same time.

Amber giggled, and Hector kissed her cheek. "I hope you'll forgive me," he said. "I'm ready to come back to Haggersmoore with you now."

"And I'm ready to stay right here with you forever if you want," Amber whispered. The bracelet he'd given her jangled as she rubbed his head.

"How touching," a gruff voice said from the doorway. Sir Guyon's armored frame blocked the sunlight.

Hector stepped away from Amber. "What do you want?"

"I want the weapon you owe me." His hand rested on his sword hilt and his face contorted in an angry frown.

"It's not my fault you didn't catch the thief who took it," Hector said.

"Oh, I think it is," Sir Guyon said. "I think you arranged to have someone take it so we wouldn't get our hands on our rightful property. I know you have. The guards out there just told me you used it to send a message to Kaal."

Before Hector could respond, another angry voice called his name from the street. He pushed past Sir Guyon and walked out to find Goldmane and the other dwarves staring down Sir Guyon's knights. Goldmane's beard was starting to grow back, and he looked recovered from his encounter with Hector's device.

"Welcome, Your Highness," Hector said, bowing and trying not to laugh. "What brings you to Kaal?"

"You know what I want, and I'm prepared to pay far more than these sniveling knights ever gave you for it."

Hector pursed his lips and glanced behind him at the mess of parts scattered over the workbench. "I'm sorry. The sandstorm destroyed my machine."

"Maybe it did," Sir Guyon said. "But you had another one here, didn't you? There had to be for your message to have worked. Where is it? I demand you hand it over."

Hector looked over at Shem, and Shem raised his eyebrows in an I-told-you-so look.

"All right, sure," Hector said. "You can both have it. It's right in there. Divide the pieces up however you like."

Goldmane stamped forward, pushed Sir Guyon out of the way, stepped into the lab, and looked around. "What?" he roared after a moment. "You took it apart?"

Hector shrugged. "It's no use now that the sandstorm buried the wire and destroyed the other device."

"But we could still use it as a weapon!" Goldmane thundered.

"Sure you can. Go right ahead. Help yourselves." Hector motioned to the workbench and walked out the door.

Sir Guyon strode over, sniffed at a beaker of acid, and lifted a stray wire. "Where are the blueprints?" he called.

"Right here." Hector tapped the side of his head. "But I'm afraid I've forgotten how I put it all together."

"Why you little . . ." Goldmane charged out of the lab and lifted Hector up by the front of his green shirt, shaking him.

Tumbleweed roared and released a spurt of flame into the air. "Put him down, or I'll tear you into little bits," he bellowed.

Goldmane dropped Hector and stalked away, motioning for the other dwarves to follow him.

Sir Guyon lingered a moment in the doorway. "Bring a crate and pack up all this stuff," he told his men. "We've paid for it, and it's ours. Maybe someday we'll be able to figure out how to put it all together."

Hector took Amber's hand while the knights set to work claiming their weapon.

A group of young people ambled down the street toward them, Syndall in the lead, followed by a lanky boy with disheveled black hair, a tall boy with flashing silver eyes and a pair of curved swords, and a pretty girl with long blonde hair.

"Hey, what's going on?" the black-haired boy said with a wide mischievous grin. "That was one angry bunch of dwarves we just passed. And wow, is that a brass dragon?"

"Mudd!" Hector cried. He'd feared he'd never see his human friend again. He raced over and shook Mudd's hand so hard the tools rattled in his apron.

"Hector," Mudd said, laughing. "We've been looking all over for you. At least ever since the silver dragon told us you were alive. I can't believe it. When we got to Purespring, Syndall volunteered to bring us out to Kaal to find you."

"Syndall," Amber said, racing over and giving Syndall a hug.

Hector pulled away from Mudd. "You talked to a silver dragon?" he said in awe.

"Oh sure. We had quite an adventure. Talked to a silver dragon, fought a red dragon, got a whole bunch of treasure. It was the best, but . . . I thought you died in the fire after saving me."

"Sorry about that," Hector said. "I think you'll be glad to know that my flying device worked."

"It got you out?"

Hector nodded. "Not too much worse for the wear, except"—he rubbed his bald head—"my hair never did grow back."

Tumbleweed sniffed the air and circled Mudd and his friends. He put his nose right up against the taller boy with the swords. "You don't smell like a human," he grumbled.

The boy flinched away from him.

"Um, Hector?" Mudd said. "Maybe some introductions are in order."

"Right," Hector said. "Mudd, this is Tumbleweed, a friend of mine. And this is Amber." Hector put his arm around Amber's shoulder.

"Hi, Tumbleweed, Amber," Mudd said, then pointed to the blonde girl. "This is my sister Hiera. I don't think you ever met her."

Hiera smiled. "Pleased to meet you, Hector. Mudd talks about you all the time, so I feel like I already know you." She grabbed Hector and lifted him into the air in a tight hug.

He gasped, and she put him back down.

"And who's this?" Tumbleweed said, still growling at the other boy.

"This is Sterling," Mudd said, pushing in between Tumbleweed and Sterling. "He's the silver dragon's son, and my friend."

Tumbleweed snuffed in surprise, stepped back, and bowed. "My apologies. I've never smelled a silver dragon before. But I was right, you aren't human."

Sterling grimaced. "Brass dragons talk too much."

Mudd laughed. "Now we're all friends, I have a question for Hector."

"What?" Hector's curiosity piqued. Mudd had come all this way just to ask him a question?

Mudd reached into his pocket and pulled out a gnomish puzzle consisting of several strands of twisted metal entangled with one another. "I bought this from a couple of gnomes in Palanthas. I know there's some way to get the metal strands apart, but I can't figure it out. It's weird. I'm good at these puzzles. I've solved every other one just like that"—Mudd snapped his fingers—"but I can't figure this one out at all."

Hector started to laugh. Mudd had a mind like a gnome's. He could unlock any door, take apart any device, and put it back together better than it was before. Poor Mudd, to come upon *this* puzzle. It must have been driving him crazy. It took all of Hector's will to stop laughing.

"S-sorry," he said, wiping his eyes.

"What's so funny?" Hiera asked.

Hector cleared his throat and took the puzzle from Mudd. "You bought this from Wig and Twig?"

Mudd nodded.

"First you have to know that they're friends of mine. Terrible jokers. Well, after they reversed one of my inventions—causing a whole cartload of pasta to explode off the roof and tomato sauce to flood the basement—I fashioned this and gave it to them. Silly fools. I see they never figured out how to get it apart, so they passed it on to you."

Mudd frowned. "They don't even know how to solve it?"

"Nope. But I do." Hector reached into his apron pocket and took out his wire cutters. With a flick of his wrist he cut one of the wires on the puzzle and all the rest fell apart in his hand.

"What?" Mudd cried. "But that's cheating."

"No. That's solving the puzzle the only possible way." Hector held up the wire cutters. "I use these to solve all kinds of problems, big and small."

Tumbleweed burst into laughter. "It's true. It's true," he chortled. His sides heaved, and he plopped down on the ground, laughing so hard his legs kicked up in the air.

Mudd spread his hands. "What's so funny?"

"Hector used those wire cutters to defeat the granddaddy of blue dragons all by himself," Tumbleweed wheezed.

Hector spun the wire cutters in his hand and shoved them back into his apron. "The fact is you can do anything you want with an imagination and a good set of tools." He gave Amber a hug. "Except, of course, show people you love them."

Mudd grinned. "I think you're right."

Amber frowned. "Hector, what about Dani? Did she catch up with you? Did she try to steal your invention?"

"Who's Dani?" Syndall asked.

Amber put her hands on her hips. "The thief who stole your parents' fabric. It was that burned girl with the wagon. She planned to steal Hector's invention next."

"Dani's not so bad," Hector said. "She was just scared and desperate. She needed a good home, and she's found one now." Hector smiled up at Tumbleweed. "Tumbleweed, this is Syndall Goodlund. I think you have something for her."

"Right." Tumbleweed got to his feet and unfastened the bundle of fabric from his back. He set it down on the road in front of Syndall.

"Oh," Syndall cried, kneeling down and running her hands over the fabric. "You got it back. Now we'll be able to sell it for enough supplies to keep the shop running. Thank you, Hector. Thank you, Tumbleweed."

"No problem," Hector said. "Tumbleweed has given me enough coin to hire a wagon to carry it back to Purespring. We can all head back there together on our way home."

"Great," Mudd said. "I'll run to the stables and arrange a wagon." He zipped away, and Hector went over to Tumbleweed. "I'm going to miss you."

Tumbleweed lowered his head and licked Hector's cheek. "I'll miss you too. Stay in touch like you promised."

"I will." With a big smile, Tumbleweed spread his wings and shot up into the air. Whooping with delight, he did three barrel rolls and then sped away over the city walls out across the desert.

About the Author

R.D. HENHAM is a scribe in the great library of Palanthas. In the course of transcribing stories of legendary dragons, the author felt a gap existed in the story of the everydragon: ordinary dragons who end up doing extraordinary things. With the help of Sindri Suncatcher and fellow scribes, R.D. has filled that gap with these books.

About the Author's Assistant

REBECCA SHELLEY has a great love for magical things, especially dragons and fairies. Her four children are her biggest fans. She has written a number of books and stories for children and adults, including assisting the writing of *Red Dragon Codex*.

ACKNOWLEDGEMENTS

R.D. Henham and I would like to give heartfelt thanks to all our readers who give us such good feedback and work so hard to find all our silly mistakes. Thank you Jessica, Richard, Catherine, Laurie, Kimberly, Bruce, Matthew, Laura Ann, Bryce, Tracy, and Holly.

Special thanks to my agent, Jennifer Cayea. She should receive a gold medal for patience and kindness. I am forever in her debt.

Big, huge thanks to our editor, Stacy Whitman. She is brilliant at transforming a story into something far better than it could be without her.

Thanks to our friend, Sindri Suncatcher, who takes all the risks to get up close and personal with the dragons, searching all over Krynn to bring their stories to light.

Thanks to my dear husband, David Shelley, who has gone out to get pizza many a night when I've been too immersed in my writing to think about important things like making dinner. His heroic efforts to keep the house running while I'm off playing with dragons deserves more praise than I can convey with words.

Rebecca Shelley
Assistant to R.D. Henham

**Fall in love with an evil baby dragon
in the next dragon codex!**

When ten-year-old Scamp Weaver finds a locked chest
in a forest clearing, he feels like his life is finally
about to change for the better.

But he doesn't bargain for just how much change the chest
will bring. Inside he finds a dragon egg and a mysterious
ancient scroll, which set Scamp and his best friend, Dannika,
off on a harrowing adventure, chased by dragon hunters
who want the contents of the chest for themselves.
Life gets ever more complicated when the baby green dragon
hatches. Will this cute, mischievous hatchling really
grow up to be an evil green dragon?

Find out in

GREEN
DRAGON CODEX

Coming June 2009

Open up a World of Adventure with The

Dungeons & Dragons®

Roleplaying Game Starter Set

Run the Game
Build your own dungeons and pit your friends against monsters and villains!

Play the Game
Explore the dungeon with your friends, fight the monsters, and bring back the treasure!

Grab some Friends
and the
Starter Set
and
Start Playing Today

dndinsider.com

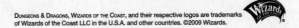